BETH JORDACHE
THE NEW JOURNALS

BETH JORDACHE
THE NEW JOURNALS

Adapted from
Phil Redmond's Brookside
by
Rachel Braverman

A CHANNEL FOUR BOOK

B■XTREE

The publishers would like to thank the following
for their help and advice in producing this book:

Phil Redmond
Philip Reevell
Brookside Producer Mal Young

First published in Great Britain in 1995 by
Boxtree Limited
Broadwall House, 21 Broadwall, London SE1 9PL

ISBN 0 7522 0765 2

10 9 8 7 6 5 4 3 2 1

A CIP catalogue entry for this book is available
from the British Library

Front cover design: Head Design
Front cover photograph: Nicky Johnston
Typeset by SX Composing Ltd, Rayleigh, Essex
Printed in Great Britain by
Cox & Wyman Ltd, Reading, Berks

16 April, 1994

If I don't tell someone soon, I'll go mad.

On the surface, everything's wonderful. Beth Jordache, medical student, loads of friends, great love life. A normal, healthy, happy girl. Not a care in the world.

But my dream's like a horror film. Mum and I on the sofa, planning to get rid of him. Putting weedkiller in his whisky. Crushing aspirins for his tea. We murdered my father.

Then that silence. The weight of him as he fell on top of me. If I close my eyes, I can still see Mum standing there, with the knife in her hand.

We had to do it. It was him or us. We had no choice.

It goes round and round in my head. I don't know why. Sometimes I forget about it for days, weeks even. There must be a trigger, something that reminds me, brings back the nightmares, but I don't know what it is.

I just have to get on with my life.

18 April, 1994

Mike Dixon next door lent me his video-camera. Typical media student, he went around for ages filming everything and everyone. He's graduated now, so he said I could borrow it for a while. I told him I wanted to make a video diary. Which is true, more or less. Not that anyone's ever going to get to see it.

I set it up in my bedroom and talked and talked. It really helped. Writing it down like this gets it out of my system a bit, but there's something about actually saying the words out loud. Making it real and at the same time stopping it from being this awful big cloud of fear.

I can't explain it properly. I suppose it's like Catholics confessing. You admit what you've done and you're forgiven.

Only there's no forgiveness for us.

What we did was a crime. If we were caught, we'd be put in prison. So would Sinbad for helping us to bury the body. What would it be? Aiding and abetting, I suppose. Never mind that he only did it because he's in love with Mum.

I don't regret what we did. Not for one moment. He made our lives hell. He deserved everything he got. We never deserved him.

That's what I told the tape. Every last detail. The truth, the whole truth and nothing but the truth.

24 April, 1994

It worked. I feel so much better. No nightmares. No dark thoughts. I can even look at the patio in peace.

Not that I've seen it lately. Chris is back! She's been in London for the last couple of weeks with friends. I couldn't believe how much I missed her! Perhaps that's why I had to make the video. Even though I can't tell her about what happened, I feel so much more secure and confident when she's around.

We've been spending most of our time together. She's the most wonderful person I've ever met. Funny and clever and stunningly attractive. And she loves me!

Well, likes me a lot.

I wish I could tell Mum I'm going out with another woman. It doesn't help that Chris is my anatomy tutor. As far as Mum's concerned, we're just good friends. It would never occur to her to think otherwise. She's dead chuffed at the thought of me, a mere medical student, hanging around with a college lecturer.

If only she knew.

If only I could tell her.

I could handle that. No problem. I'm proud of what I am. Why should I be ashamed of being gay? But I'm terrified she'll take it the wrong way.

It's brilliant staying around at hers. Breakfast's just amazing. Filter coffee and fresh croissants from this little patisserie round the corner. This morning, I watched her reading the papers in bed. It was fascinating! First, she read the news, then the review bit, then the magazine, like it was dessert. The business pages went straight into the recycling box.

I'd much rather be with her than some scuzzy student. They're pathetically immature. The posh ones go on and on about how much money Mummy and Daddy have to give them. The poor ones whinge about working Saturdays in a dry cleaners. Everyone moans about the price of drinks. Chris never moans about anything. She's the most positive person I've ever met.

All her pictures are properly framed and they're authentic prints, not reproductions. I'm still at the stage of tacky posters on the wall, with smudges on the corners from the Blu-tack. I guess at heart, I'm a student like any other.

Hardly anyone knows I'm gay. Just Chris and one or two others. I ought to come out properly. I'm too used to secrets, too used to keeping all the important things in my life hidden. I feel safest when nobody knows anything about me.

25 April, 1994

This place is getting like a hotel. Sinbad practically lives here. Not that I mind him being around. He's great for Mum. Just what she needs. Someone funny and reliable and ordinary. Someone who loves her. Someone who wouldn't dream of raising his hand to her.

Now his mother's moved in. Ruth's alright. She's been ill and she needs somewhere to stay. The extension's on the ground floor, so it makes sense for her to come here. Actually, it's hard to remember she's in the house, sometimes. She's incredibly polite and retiring. Mum does loads for her, but she never asks. The perfect house guest, really.

Mum asked me if I minded — once she'd moved in!

What was I supposed to say? Get rid of her now, this minute? As if! Besides, she caught me just as Chris turned into the Close. Hardly the right time to start a discussion.

Chris and Mum want to meet each other. I'm trying desperately to put them off. Mum's got it into her head that I'm ashamed of her. I hate her thinking that. If only she knew! If only she *did* know. I'd love to tell her about me and Chris, but I don't have a clue how she'd react. The word LESBIAN's never been so much as whispered in this house. Eventually, I had to agree to bringing Chris round. Sometime. In the VERY distant future.

I couldn't believe it! When I got into the car, Chris said exactly the same thing. Was I ashamed of her? I was terrified that Mum would come out and there'd be an embarrassing cosy chat on the kerbside.

Chris thinks Mum sounds nice.

Mum thinks Chris sounds nice.

I'm not going to be able to keep them apart for long.

1 May, 1994

Rachel's being a complete brat. Why does she have to play the part of grotty little sister the whole time? Whingeing and whining and making snide comments about Chris. She doesn't know we're a couple, of course. But I'm sick of hearing her going on about me being 'teacher's pet'.

I know exactly what's got into her. It's because of that Lee, who's moved in next door. Rachel's really gone on him. Personally, I can't see what's so special about him. He's tall and skinny and unbelievably shy. Never has a word to say for himself. As for the spots. . . .

Nothing round here's ever straightforward. It turns out that mild-mannered Lee Banks spent two years in a youth detention centre for joyriding. Apparently, he knocked this little girl over and now she's stuck in a wheelchair.

SCANDAL!
SHOCK HORROR!!

The Brookside Residents Association – chairman David 'Bing' Crosbie – have made the whole family's life a misery. They actually had a meeting about it. What did they expect to do? Drum them out of town?

They're so reactionary. As far as they're concerned, hanging's too good for him. Never mind that he's been punished. Never mind that he didn't set out to ruin someone's life. He's not welcome in our respectable little enclave.

WE DON'T WANT HIS KIND ROUND HERE!!!

Of course, when Mum found out, she banned Rachel from seeing Lee. If she wasn't in love with him before, she will be now. Forbidden passion and all that. No doubt they're sneaking off together every chance they get.

If Mum's this worried about Rachel going out with Lee, what on earth would she think about me and Chris?

3 May, 1994

A disastrous day!

We were all supposed to be going out. Sinbad had arranged to take Mum, Rachel and Ruth off somewhere and Chris and I were going to hang around New Brighton. Alone at last!

Chris turned up five minutes early. She landed on the doorstep with Sinbad. He comes in, so, of course, she does too. I'd wanted to be ready and waiting when she arrived, but what with Rachel whingeing and Mum fussing, I still hadn't got my boots on.

Mum made the most of the opportunity, of course. She whipped the kettle on and started making small talk. It was completely embarrassing! Chris lapped it up. She's got a thing about playing happy families. Like she joins in, but at the same time she's sort of laughing at all these 'ordinary' people. Sometimes, I think she's got a weird sense of humour.

I hate introducing my friends to my family. It's so embarrassing. Mum always treats me like I'm about ten! A bit of me wanted to make an announcement:-

'CHRIS IS MY GIRLFRIEND. WE'RE LESBIANS. WE GO OUT TOGETHER, HAVE FUN TO-GETHER, SLEEP TOGETHER.

'Now, how about that cup of tea?'

Most of me just wanted to get out of there as quickly as possible.

Just as I thought I'd got Chris moving, Ruth's door opened. There she was, still in her dressing-gown, looking like death warmed up. She didn't feel up to going out! Great! So then there's a discussion about what the other three are going to do. Mum and Sinbad vie with each other to be the biggest martyr.

Then Mum has a brilliant idea. Why doesn't Rachel tag along with Beth and Chris? I can think of a hundred reasons why not, starting with the fact that she's being a complete pain at the moment. But Mum mouths 'please' at me and she has that trapped look on her face, so I have to agree. Chris doesn't mind. She just says there is plenty of room in the car and Rach would be welcome. Which goes to show she doesn't know my little sister!

As soon as everything is settled, Rachel has to go to the shops to stock up with chocolate. Another delay! While she's gone, Mum and Chris make all these great plans for Chris to come to tea one day next week. I could have died!

The one good thing was that Sinbad had a private word with me. Chris is 'very nice', according to him. He knows the score. I suppose he was the first person I came out to. Thank goodness I can rely on one sympathetic ear.

We finally pile into Chris' car, leaving Mum and Sinbad to a cosy tête-à-tête over a takeaway. At the edge of the Close, Rachel suddenly shrieks 'Stop the car. Stop the car.' Chris braked so hard I nearly went through the windscreen.

Who should step out of the bushes? Lee Banks. I might have guessed. Rachel must have persuaded him to come along when she went to the shops.

I didn't want him to come, but when Chris found out they weren't supposed to see each other, she thought it was dead romantic. Sometimes, she's no help!

The car journey was horrible. No-one said a word. I sat there, feeling like a twelve-year-old, who's gone out for a treat with Miss. Lee and Rachel were holding hands in the back.

It was better once we got there. The fair's loads of fun. In fact, having Lee along was an advantage. The young lovers headed for the dodgems, leaving us older lovers alone at last.

Even when they'd gone, I couldn't relax. I had visions of Mum passing the sausage rolls and making meaningful remarks about boyfriends. The trouble is, Chris came out ages ago. I think she's forgotten how difficult it is.

She said she'd never met anyone who takes things as hard as I do. I suppose she's right. But when I tried to apologize, she told me to stop saying sorry all the time. Can't I do anything right?

There wasn't a Tunnel of Love, but we did have a laugh necking in the Ghost Train.

We were having a great time, until the gruesome twosome showed up again. They'd managed to get through all their money in about half an hour. The only way we could stop them hanging around with us was for Chris to give them a tenner.

Rachel's such a wind-up merchant. I could strangle her sometimes. She does it on purpose.

Chris and I went back to the seafront, where we'd parked the car. It was completely deserted. Chris put her arm round me. I was a bit uncomfortable at first, but she's completely irresistible. I'd never kissed a woman in broad daylight before. And certainly not in a 2CV!

But when I came up for air I spotted Rachel in the rear-view mirror running towards the car. She stopped suddenly and Lee caught her up.

She must have seen us!

I know she did!

The journey back was worse than going out. Silence again, but I could feel Rachel's eyes on the back of my neck. When we got home, she said, 'Good bye' and 'Thanks for taking us' to Chris in that awful, sarcastic, mocking way she has.

She hasn't said a word to me since.

What am I going to do if she tells Mum?

4 May, 1994

I didn't sleep a wink last night. I went over and over what happened.

Timetable of events:

Midnight to 2:00 a.m.	I am convinced Rachel has already told Mum. I lie there, waiting for the knock at the door, half-expecting to be hauled out of bed and sent packing.
2:00 a.m. to 4:00 a.m.	I think maybe – just maybe – Rachel didn't see anything. Maybe we'll get away with it.
4:00 a.m. to 4.01 a.m.	It crosses my mind that Rachel saw what happened and doesn't mind. She understands and is sympathetic.
4:01 a.m. to 6.00 a.m.	Reality breaks in. The most likely scenario is that Rachel caught us snogging, but hasn't said anything. Yet.

I got up then, too exhausted to stay in bed any longer. Breakfast was a nightmare. Mum didn't notice anything wrong. She was in a really good mood with me for having taken Rachel out for a treat. Rachel just gave me this look. A straight, I-know-your-secret stare. Then she escaped. No doubt to discuss my private life with Lee Banks.

When she came back, she shut herself in her room. I found her sprawled on the bed, reading *Viz*. She was really defensive about it, but I was hardly in a position to put on the big sister act.

I said I needed to talk about what she might have seen in the car.

'Me?' she said, eyes all big and innocent. 'I didn't see anything.'

I almost danced with relief.

'Apart from you snogging your teacher,' she went on.

I wasn't going to deny it. What's the point? Then she really laid into me. Called me a 'dirty lesbo' and said she thought it was disgusting kissing girls. And, of course, she threatened to tell. It was easy for her to work out Mum doesn't know. She'd hardly be inviting Chris round to tea if she did!

I said I'd tell about her and Lee if she breathed a word. She just laughed. What's Mum going to be more bothered about? Her and Lee with their normal, adolescent hormones? Or me and Chris?

The only way I could get her to keep her mouth shut was to promise to persuade Mum to let her see Lee. Blackmailed by a stupid little kid sister. She doesn't care about Mum. If she did, she'd keep her big mouth shut and leave me to make my own decisions.

5 May, 1994

I went round to Lee's this afternoon. Rosie, his

Mum, was out in the front garden. It's not fair the way the neighbours treat them. In a nosy neighbourhood like ours, you really feel it if people ignore you.

All I can say is that she showed me a different side to my horrible sister. According to Rosie, Rachel brought Lee out of himself. Put a smile on his face!

Rachel!

Whinger of whingers. Sulking supremo.

She almost managed to convince me that Rachel was one of the good guys. If she can do that, she can do anything, so I persuaded her to come round to talk to Mum.

Poor Mum! She was quite embarrassed. I suppose she was just trying to protect Rachel. Frankly, I should think Lee would need protecting from her!

Rosie made a brilliant speech.

'Lee's really upset, you know,' she said. 'He thinks the world of Rachel. It's the first bit of happiness he's had since they locked him away. Now, he feels like he's being punished all over again. He's paid a price for what he did. God, listen to me. I'm talking as if he's a mass murderer. He was twelve years of age. He's still only a kid now. Has he got to carry this lot round with him for the rest of his life?'

Actually, I agreed with her. I could see Mum was changing her mind, but all she'd say was that she'd consider it. When Rosie left, there was a scurrying sound on the stairs. No doubt young Rach was listening in for all she was worth. I would have.

6 May, 1994

Mum reminded me that it's exactly a year since we did it. She should try not to think about it. I don't. Most of the time.

I told her I don't have a note of killing my dad in my diary.

7 May, 1994

Rachel's been a model of good behaviour! Sort of. Peeling spuds and smarming fit to bust. Mum's more-or-less decided that she *can* see Lee. It hardly took any persuasion from me. Not that I'll let my grotty little sister know that!

She doesn't deserve it. God, the crap she came out with this evening! I could have killed her. She went on and on about how her and her mates were talking about Lesbians in the playground.

It was unbelievable! Being around Chris and her friends, I sometimes forget how homophobic the rest of the world is. Perhaps I should spend one lunchtime a month back at school to remind me!

There's one of Rachel's mates – Chantelle – who's a real know-all. She sees half a programme on the TV and thinks she's an expert on the subject.

Chantelle says Lesbians are fat.

Chantelle says Lesbians shave their heads.

Chantelle says Lesbians hate men.

But *Rachel* thinks they look normal.

What does Mum think?

I was so scared, I cut myself with the potato peeler. At least, it stopped the conversation!

Mum asked me about it later on. Did I think Rachel has a crush on a woman teacher? Was she mixing with the 'wrong' kind of girl? How's she going to turn out, given all that she's been through? Will she never be able to look a man in the face – or elsewhere – again?

Well, she certainly doesn't have to worry about Rachel. You only have to see her and Lee, hormones a-poppin'. No confusion there!

Rachel's little jibes actually did me a favour. They gave me a chance to have a proper talk to Mum about it. I had this sort of daydream that I'd tell her about me and Chris and she'd give me a hug and say it was OK.

A daydream, but you never know. . . .

I said I had gay friends at university and asked Mum if she'd be mortally offended if I brought one of them home. I didn't say on what basis! She said if they're friends of mine, that's good enough for her.

Then, I asked her what she'd do if someone she knew came out to her. Mum didn't want to answer that one. Wanted to know why I was asking.

Just curious.

She said she'd do her best to try and understand what that person was going through.

I was dead relieved. Maybe Mum will be OK about it. Trouble was, we'd been so deep in conversation, we didn't notice the milk boiling over. By the time we'd cleaned up the mess, the moment had passed.

Mum must have told Rachel the good news about her and Lee. She actually came to thank me. Not that her thanks mean very much. I told her to keep her mouth shut about me and Chris, but she wouldn't promise. It all depends on what's in it for her.

9 May, 1994

We're in trouble.
Money!
The root of all evil.

Not to mention a £90 phone bill. Mum was livid. I haven't seen her in such a rage for ages. Rachel copped it for hour-long conversations with Chantelle. She sees her every day in school. Heaven knows what they find to talk about in the evenings.

Admittedly, there were a couple of longish calls to Chris. But when she was down in London last month, she couldn't very well take advantage of her friend's phone. I *had* to ring her back. It's easy to get carried away when you're in love! And expensive. From now on, the phone's been made 999 calls only. We can make as many as we like of them – they're free.

When the milkman called, Mum made us duck down and hide. She owes two weeks and hadn't got a penny on her. It was dead humiliating! I never realized things had got that bad.

I said I'd put towards the phone bill from my grant. God knows how, though. I've got an overdraft already. Not to mention a student loan hanging over my head. I haven't told Mum I'm in debt. She's got enough on her plate without me going on about how I can't afford to stay on at uni.

13 May, 1994

Friday the thirteenth. Unlucky for some.
Like Rachel, if she pushes her luck any further.
I'm getting sick and tired of her endless little digs and snide comments. She's blackmailing me. The snotty little kid's blackmailing me!

This evening she wanted me and Chris to take her and Lee to the pictures. Of course, I said 'no'. Who wants to spend time with a couple of adolescents necking in the back row? Particularly when we want to be snogging ourselves.

Mum was with Ruth at the time, taking her supper in. Rachel called out to her and I just knew she was going to tell. Mum comes rushing in, dead irritated. Miss Sweetness-And-Light asks her if she wants any bread and butter made. Butter that wouldn't melt in her mouth!

Chris wasn't exactly chuffed when she saw the gruesome twosome. Made some sarky comment about being a taxi service. She's much better at handling them than me, though. We'd planned to see *Romeo's Bleeding*.

Then, Rachel announced that was what she and Lee were going to see too.

Chris was brilliant! She told them that if they tried to get tickets, she'd shout at the top of her voice that they aren't even old enough to get into a 15. So off they trotted to see some kids' stuff, good as gold.

She's not afraid of anything. I wish I could be like that. So confident and sure that she's right.

Chris is getting really hacked off. I think she might finish with me if I don't do something soon. It's been a long time since she's been someone's terrible dark secret. Being held to ransom by some obnoxious teenager gets right up her nose. And I quote.

It's all such a mess!

Clean it up. That's what Chris said. Just clean it up.

15 May, 1994

Chris came over to Sunday tea today. It was as bad as I thought it would be. Rachel was being treacherously over-polite. Mum only brought out the baby pictures.

It was bad enough with Mum rattling on, without Chris taking the mick. She was just egging her on. There's this awful snap of me in a frilly, pink dress, aged four. I'm holding a balloon and I've got this disgusting smug expression on my face.

Mum went on about how much I loved that outfit. Chris caught my eye. She was virtually spitting out her sausage roll with laughter. Honestly! As if it wasn't embarrassing enough. She could have a bit of sympathy.

It got more dangerous after that. Mum wanted to know if Chris had a boyfriend tucked away. I lost my head and said she had an on-and-off relationship with some fella.

Chris wasn't too happy with me after that! Can't say I blame her. It's bad enough with Rachel giving poisonous little digs the whole time without me panicking every time relationships are mentioned. But I can't help it! I get really scared something's going to come out before I'm ready. Lying about someone else's life is pretty appalling. I wish I hadn't gone and said anything. I promised Chris it won't happen again.

Knowing my luck, Mum'll find out about us just when Chris gets fed up and dumps me.

18 May, 1994

Mum's in an incredible amount of debt! She's behind with the gas, the electricity, the phone. Everything. Even the water rates.

Then there's this stupid loan she's got to pay off to that ex-cell mate of Dad's, who was sniffing around last year. Why she and Sinbad didn't just tell him to do one, I don't know. So now, they're stuck with this massive debt to pay off. No bank or building society would give a school cleaner and a window-cleaner a legit personal loan. You've got to have money in the first place to get proper credit! So they end up with this really dodgy one-man-band outfit. Kenny Maguire comes round every week with his heavy to collect the payments. Always so polite, but you know he could turn nasty if he didn't get what he came for.

Mum asked me if I could get a student loan to help out. I hated having to say no. I had to admit I'd already got one. What else could I do? My grant's a pittance. Books alone cost a fortune.

It's not as if I'm the only one. There's loads of people in our year up to their eyes in debt. I haven't told her about the overdraft. It's over £1,000.

I thought Mum would be furious, but she said she was proud of me sorting myself out. I got off to uni before she could go all slushy on me.

Looks like we're all going to have to tighten our belts for a while. Anyway, my exams are coming up, so I'm going to have to stay late to revise. At least, it'll stop me spending money.

20 May, 1994

Max Farnham from across the Close asked if I'd babysit for him and his wife last night. Good timing or what! Just when I need the money. He said that it could be a regular thing. He's not bad – for a yuppie – and Patricia's really nice. It's hard to believe she's the daughter of the dreaded David Crosbie. He's prejudiced about everything and she's really tolerant. When I was going out with Margaret, Patricia was fine about it. And Margaret was her nanny!

I couldn't resist it. The Farnhams were going out for some posh meal, so they weren't going to be back till dead late. I phoned Chris to come over and join me.

Chris brought a bottle of wine. The kid was in bed. Perfect. We snuggled up on the black leather sofa for a cosy evening in. We weren't up to much. Just snogging. Enjoying a little quality time, as they say.

Suddenly, there was this absolute roar. David Crosbie had only let himself in! God knows why. Talk about catching us at it. My blouse was half-undone and Chris's hair was all over the place.

He went berserk. Completely mad. Called us every name under the sun and chucked us out. Chris just said he was narrow-minded and I shouldn't worry about what he says.

It's all very well for her. Quite apart from the money, what am I going to do if he tells Mum?

I spent most of the night worrying and the morning watching for him at the window. I told Sinbad what had happened and he said I should go and apologize. It *was* a bit out of order inviting someone round like that, I suppose. Boyfriend or girlfriend.

It was horrible, but quite funny when I got there. David's wife, Jean, is great. She'd chucked him out because he was being such a bigot. He was standing there on the doorstep, pleading with her through the letter-box.

I told him I was sorry about what happened. He

wouldn't accept it. Said I ought to be bloody well ashamed of myself and that he'd never seen anything so disgusting. Then he said he was sure my mother would be appalled if she knew about my abhorrent behaviour.

My heart just plummeted. I thought he was bound to let on. But he said he wouldn't, as long as it doesn't happen again. It was a relief. Sort of.

I've got to tell Mum. Too many other people know. Too many dangerous people. I'd hate her to be the last one to be told.

25 May, 1994

Welcome to Hotel Jordache! Whenever I want to catch Mum on her own, there's always someone in the way. Ruth's quite demanding. The operation left her very frail and Mum's had to do a lot of looking after her. She's great like that – really gentle and caring. Besides, it makes Sinbad even more fond of her. Not that Mum does it for that reason. I *never* mind Sinbad popping in and out. If only the two of them would get it together properly!

It's Rachel I could do without. She's always there with her stupid, childish comments about her 'friend called *LES*'. She's such a fascist! Why does she have to be so horrible? Why is she determined to make things even harder for me? I went out of my way so she could carry on seeing Lee and this is how she thanks me.

I told her to give me a bit more space or else . . . It

seems to have worked a bit. She hasn't been quite such a stroppy cow for the past few days.

It won't last. As soon as I find the right moment, I'm going to tell Mum.

31 May, 1994

Lee Banks' big brother, Carl, has turned up again. I could live without that. Last time he was around, he had a thing with Margaret. The slimy git. Never mind the fact that he's married. Or that Marge was really vulnerable. He simply took advantage. It was so unfair on her. We'd just split up and she'd decided going out with me had been an aberration. A blip in normality! She was desperate to prove how straight she was by going to bed with the first bloke to come along.

Carl's been going round with Mike Dixon, who's obviously not a good judge of character! Shame really. Mike's a nice bloke. Anyway, he and Carl invited me and Chris to this spur-of-the-moment barbecue. A party, Mike said, before his finals start. A few neighbours and some of Mike's college mates.

Talk about a set up! We got there and guess what, we were the only guests. Lambs to the slaughter. I'm surprised they didn't sling us on the barbie and serve us up with mint sauce. Carl tried chatting me up and Mike was talking to Chris.

Actually, they got on well. Mike was telling her about the video he made for his course. These media types! So we went inside and watched it. I thought it was excellent. So did Chris. Some of the images were really powerful. I never knew Mike had it in him. Carl, of course, preferred all-action Arnie.

The lads steered the conversation round to boy-friends and that. Carl wanted to know who I went to the cinema with. I said I went with Chris. She was sitting in an armchair and I was on the arm. I could feel her hand against my leg, sort of giving me courage. It was amazing!

I told them I don't have a boyfriend. I go out with Chris.

It was worth it just to see the look on their faces. Gobsmacked isn't the word!

Carl was totally pathetic about it, naturally, but Mike was OK. Even though he was completely amazed, he wanted to know about it. To understand what I was going through. I didn't mind explaining. It kind of brought us a bit closer. Like he really knows who I am now – and still wants to be my friend!

Chris had the final word, though. Carl asked how she knew she wasn't straight underneath it all. Out came the cliché – maybe she just hasn't found the right fella. So she said how did he know *he* wasn't gay. Maybe *he's* the one who hasn't found Mr. Right.

I've never seen anybody go so red!

3 June, 1994

Ruth's announced she's emigrating to Australia! Just when I thought we were stuck with her for life. Apparently, she's got a brother out there with a family and a job. Everything's perfect!

The trouble is – she's invited Sinbad to go too. He doesn't know what to do. Hanging around the kitchen while Mum goes on about what a great opportunity it is and how wonderful it'll be for him to be with his own relations. It's perfectly obvious she's trying to hide what she's feeling.

Why doesn't Sinbad get the message?

Why won't Mum just tell him she loves him and ask him to stay?

She's miserable.

He's miserable.

Honestly, the pair of them are driving me mad!

7 June, 1994

I babysat for Patricia again last night. She's really cool about me being gay. Thank goodness for people like her and Jean. Between the pair of them, they keep David Crosby under control. If there's any 'appalling behaviour' going on, it's his, not mine!

Patricia said she'd been gobsmacked when Margaret told her about us. It didn't make her feel any differently towards her, though. Live and let live, was how she put it. She said that once she'd got over the shock, she just wanted Margaret to get on with whatever made her happy.

Will Mum be like that?

Of course, she wants me to be happy, but what does that mean? Doing what comes naturally, or doing what's so-called normal? Even Chris had problems with her parents. They're fine about it now, but it took her a long time.

I've been thinking about Marge a lot. I really did love her and she loved me. I'm sure she did. It was just that she wasn't comfortable with it. Always keeping it a deep, dark secret. Never wanting to tell a living soul. As though she were ashamed of herself and ashamed of me.

I felt so *rejected*.

I've just realized – this must be how Chris feels when I refuse to tell Mum.

As though I'm ashamed of myself and ashamed of her!

I haven't seen very much of Chris lately. She keeps going on about me concentrating on my exams rather than my social life at the moment.

10 June, 1994

If Mum doesn't do something soon, she's going to lose Sinbad. And he's the best thing that's ever happened to her. Everything's going really fast. The plane tickets are here. Ruth and Sinbad have started packing – the living room's a departure lounge, full of boxes and suitcases. Ruth's *and* Sinbad's.

Mum got a shock when she saw them. She's *got* to tell him how she feels. If she doesn't, he's going to be 10,000 miles away, chatting up the first Sheila that comes along. Why won't she at least talk to him and let him decide with her? It's obvious they've got feelings for each other, but all they do these days is make stupid comments about the weather.

We met up with him on the Parade this afternoon. Mum completely bottled out. Instead of saying how much she'd miss him – how much she needs him and wants him to stay around – she just said he wasn't to worry about the loan when he'd gone. She actually said we can manage fine on our own!

I couldn't believe it!

She's so screwed up about everything she got him involved in. What with Him out there in the garden and that bloody loan-shark coming round every two minutes. She thinks she's doing Sinbad a favour by letting him go.

Sinbad's face dropped. There's no way he wants to go. Can't she see how unhappy she'd making him?

I made an excuse to go back and have a word with him myself. He's going round to see her this afternoon.

11 June, 1994

It worked! Sinbad's staying!!

It's not only brilliant – it's dead funny, too. Both of them took me aside to tell me the good news, so I think I've been able to piece together what happened. They're acting like lovesick teenagers. Rachel and Lee – never mind me and Chris – are nothing to them!

Apparently, Sinbad caught Mum in the garden hanging out the washing. She went straight into her 'I'm so awful' routine. How scared she is of loving anyone after Dad. How she doesn't know if she could 'be physical' with a man again. Even though she's got feelings for him, she might never be able to have a proper relationship with him.

She said she didn't want him to grow old hating her because she couldn't love him properly.

Dad did that to her. Sapped her of all her self-confidence. Drained the life out of her.

Sinbad's such a hero. He stood on that patio and told her sex isn't everything in a friendship. But she still said he ought to go. Spurned and rejected, the window-cleaner turned to go. He passed into the kitchen, lingering by those dear, familiar kitchen cabinets until . . .

In a romantic whirlwind, Mum rushes in and flings herself at him. She said she suddenly realized how stupid she was being. Throwing away the best chance of happiness she'd ever had, because she was too frightened to take it.

It all came out!

Sinbad said it was the best moment of his life. He'd been feeling so hurt and lonely, knowing she probably almost loves him, but not enough to ask him to stay. Now, here she was practically on her knees begging.

Funny really, it may have been one of the most dignified moments of her life. Instead of beating around the bush and half-saying things in a half-whisper, she just said it clearly and directly.

'I do want you to stay. Please. I don't want to lose you. I don't want you to leave me. Will you stay?'

I know that's exactly what she said, because *both* of them told me.

We got a Chinese takeaway to celebrate. The two of them would have been sharing chopsticks if they could! Even Rachel was pleased. Ruth is as well, which just goes to prove what a nice woman she is. She wants what's best for her son and she likes Mum.

After supper, Ruth went back to the extension to finish packing, Rachel went off to Lee's and I went to stay with Chris. I was half hoping to find Sinbad had spent the night with Mum, but perhaps that's too much to expect at this stage.

15 June, 1994

Another abortive attempt to tell Mum about me and Chris!

Sinbad and Mum went to take Ruth to the airport. I

knew they'd be away for hours, so Chris and I sneaked into the house to have a cosy afternoon alone. My exams start in ten days and I reckoned it would do me more good to relax than to make my head spin with endless revision.

It felt a bit funny. Us being there like that, when Mum doesn't even know we're going out with each other. It was the first time I'd ever been with someone in her house. I always thought it would be with a boy-friend. Someone Mum would know dead well and like.

My sheets will never be the same again! Chris always smells wonderful. I bury my head in the pillow and breathe her in.

Afterwards, we had a bath together. Made a complete mess of the bathroom. It took us ages to mop up all the water. Chris dried my hair for me. It felt fantastic! Dead sensual.

Just as I was really getting into it, Mum and Sinbad showed up. We'd completely forgotten the time! Talk about panic. I shouted down that we were getting ready to go out. No problem. They just think we're happy little girlies glamming up to go clubbing. Preparing to attract the lads.

. It was completely ridiculous. The whole situation. I decided there and then that tonight was the night. Mum and Sinbad were off to a party at La Luz. It was the Crosbies' 40th wedding anniversary.

Fancy being married to Bing for four whole decades. I wouldn't have been able to manage 40 minutes!

It wasn't exactly the ideal situation, but Mum was in

a good mood. Besides, I couldn't stand another close shave. I'd really worked myself up to telling her, then when I got to the party, she was nowhere to be seen.

What a waste!

In a way, I was quite relieved, though. I'm going to leave it until my exams are over. Nothing's going to happen before then. The evening wasn't a complete waste though – me and Chris ended up grabbing a quick snog in the tunnel by the club.

19 June, 1994

Chris has asked me to go away with her. For the whole summer. Just the two of us, touring around Europe. Everywhere. We spent the whole evening with maps and timetables and stuff. Not that we really decided anything. Chris has been everywhere at least once and I've never left the country, so there wasn't one special place for us to go.

Just think! A month or even six weeks of the two of us. Alone together in Paris. Going up the Eiffel Tower, seeing the Mona Lisa. Or Berlin.

I was a bit worried about money, but Chris said if we stayed in hostels, it won't cost a fortune. She'll lend me the money if I'm short. Which I will be. No rush to pay her back.

She's the most wonderful person I've ever met. Gentle and tender and totally understanding. And she likes me. Really likes me. I know I'm in love with her.

I've never been so happy in my life. It feels so right, being with her. Whether we're gassing on for hours or not saying a word. Like if she's marking essays and I'm revising, it's perfect just being in the same room together.

I'm learning such a lot from her. Real things about how the world works. She's not into talking about clothes and all action films the whole time. We spend hours discussing politics and religion. Putting the world to rights. She's read everything. When I get a chance, I'm going to go through her entire bookshelves.

Maybe if things work out this summer, we could end up sharing permanently. It's almost scary – thinking we might have a future together.

21 June, 1994

Mum's found out about us!

I spent the night with Chris, like I've done loads of times before. At first, I didn't even realize anything was wrong. I told her about Chris inviting me to go on holiday with her. Mum wasn't exactly keen, but I thought she was just being a bit over-protective.

It must have taken her hours to pluck up the courage to talk about it. When she did, you'd've thought the roof had blown off. She saw us kissing outside La Luz the other night. God knows how! Someone must have told her we were there. Either that, or she was spying on us. Rachel swore blind it wasn't her. I don't know who I can and can't trust any more!

We ended up rowing about it. All day long, whenever we weren't being interrupted by Rachel or the phone or the debt collector. Exactly what I didn't want to happen. I thought it would be alright. I thought at least she'd *try* to understand. She won't though. She actually said she didn't want to.

What she did want to know is why I'd 'turned out' this way. As if it was some terrible crime. She went on and on about Chris. About all the times she'd been round here. How she used to think she was so nice. How she used to feel safe knowing I was with her.

And all the time she's a. . . . .

The word was too much for her. Lesbian. It wouldn't come out of her mouth.

I really thought it would be OK. Mum's always been there for me. Why not now? When I went out with that revolting Peter Harrison, she was so sympathetic. But just because it's another woman, she turns her back on me. There's nothing she can say to change the way I feel.

In the end, I picked up my overnight bag and went straight back to Chris. Who *did* understand. Who always understands what I'm going through.

We talked for hours and hours. I found out loads about her. She's had all the rows and the misunderstandings and the guilt. Exactly the same. It was such a relief to have someone around who's been through the same thing.

I wish I could tell her about Dad. I'm sure that's what Mum thinks this is all about.

22 June, 1994

Chris persuaded me to go back home. If I leave now, I may never get back together with Mum. I sat in the living room, trying to revise. Actually, I was just holding the book up in front of my face, waiting for Mum to come back. I didn't read a word.

We were about to have a real discussion, when water started dripping into the kitchen. There's a leak somewhere. Suddenly, there was a huge puddle on the floor. Forget emotional traumas. This was a real emergency.

It was quite funny in a way. And a relief. Mum said Sinbad was out, so she called a plumber. We spent the afternoon catching drips in the washing-up bowl. I started to tell her about the people in the flat above Chris. They let their bath overflow once and the whole ceiling came down on her bed. Then I saw Mum's face, all tense and worried. But I can't not talk about Chris. She's part of my life now. A major part.

I tried to explain, but Mum just can't see it. She's convinced it's all because of Dad – not to mention Peter Harrison turning out to be a first class rat! As far as she's concerned , I'm playing around pretending to be something I'm not because I'm scared of getting involved with another man.

Chris got the blame, of course. Mum thinks she seduced me, that she put ideas into my head. She even asked me if the university knows Chris is gay. As if it would make any difference!

I tried to tell her that if anyone did the seducing, it was me. Mum really went up the wall at that. It's like if there'd been someone before Chris, she can't go on denying the truth. I wanted to tell her about Margaret and me. That the supposedly happy, innocent, girlish friendship was much, much more. It's awful! Mum thinks that Marge and me is a perfect example of why I'm *not* gay.

I bottled out.

Now, I really wish I hadn't. When Mum asked me straight whether there had been anyone before Chris, I lost my nerve. I said she was the first. I lied because I couldn't face her anger and worry and disappointment.

The plumber finally came round and fixed the leak. I was quite glad of the distraction. When he'd gone, I escaped to my room. Revising was useless. This couldn't have happened at a worse time! At this rate, I'll flunk all my papers and be thrown out of uni. The words just kept swimming round the page.

Mum came to find me. At least, she'd stopped being angry. She wanted to know if Chris and I hold hands. I told her we did.

And kiss.

And sleep together.

Poor Mum. She doesn't understand, but she wants to. What worries her is that I'm going to get hurt. As if being with a man would keep me safe! She's so desperate to protect me from everything. Especially Dad. I can't make her see that it's got nothing to do with him. Out came all the old clichés. What happens when I wake up ten years down the line and realize it was just a phase?

I never thought how much it would destroy *her* hopes. It never even entered my head! Mum told me how when it was bad with Dad, she used to dream about my wedding day. How it would be better for me. How she'd make my wedding dress.

She's got my life mapped out now. Lying all the time about what I am. Coping with the prejudice. Landing up as the weird women down the road who lives with her butch friend and ten cats. The one the kids laugh at and everybody feels sorry for.

Why does it all have to be so tragic? If only I had her support. The worst thing is that she blames herself. As if she went wrong somewhere. As if *I* did.

23 June, 1994

I don't know how much longer I can stand the atmosphere here. Mum looks at me like I'm a freak she should feel sorry for. All this what-have-I-done-to-you business gets right up my nose.

Right now, the last thing we need is for *us* to be quarrelling. That revolting Kenny Maguire's been round again. Every time I see him, the hairs on the back of my neck rise. He's got the most horrible hand-shake of anyone I've ever come across. He sort of grips your hand in both of his – dead firm – and soaks you with slime from his palms. Ugh! I can't bear him any-where near me.

I don't trust his voice either. It's deliberately slow and soft, as if he's always talking to someone who's not all there. He comes out with these technical financial terms, so you think he's explained everything really clearly. Only afterwards, it's hard to remember exactly what he *did* say.

He was in the kitchen with Mum when I came back this afternoon. Bending over her while she signed some piece of paper. Apparently, it's a new loan agreement. His firm (which basically means *him*) takes on all Mum's debts, including the loan to him, and lumps them altogether. Mum only has to worry about one re-payment a month and that's not too outrageous.

It sounds too good to be true. I asked Mum whether she'd read the small print. She said yes, but she's in such a mood, I'm not sure. She's so trusting. Especially where smooth-talking men in suits are concerned.

I just wish she'd let me see the paper before she signed it. I have a feeling it could mean real trouble . . .

24 June, 1994

I haven't got anything left to say to Mum. We go round and round the subject of Chris, but we never get anywhere. There's like this huge gulf and we're trying to shout across it. But our voices don't carry.

Chris invited me to go down to London with her to meet some of her friends. There's this anti-Nazi demo on Sunday we're going to. That's what's so great about Chris – she really *cares* what's going on in the world. Not like most of the idiots at uni. As long as they know where their next party is coming from, they couldn't give a toss.

Why can't Mum see how good for me she is? She liked her before. When my friend was a lecturer, she was dead proud. Why is it so awful when my friend turns out to be my lover?

We had to go through the whole thing again when I told Mum I'd be away over the weekend. Mum said it was like Chris had put some kind of a spell on me. So now she's a witch, as well as a lesbian. Then she went for the emotional punch and practically begged me to stay at home and 'think things through'. As if I could somehow persuade myself to fancy men!

I'm going to have to face it – if Mum can't accept what I am, there's no point in talking about it any more. I may as well move in with Chris. Permanently.

This couldn't have come at a worse time. I've got my anatomy exam in an hour. Instead of my last-minute revision, I had to write this down to get it out of my system. God knows how I'm going to concentrate.

25 June, 1994

My own mother's ruined everything! My whole career!

I got to the exam room and Chris was invigilating. I thought that had to be a good omen. It was brilliant having her there. Every time I looked up, she caught my eye and grinned. Like she knew I could pass easily.

I would have, too. Maybe I hadn't done as much revision as I should, but all the things I'd done properly came up. Suddenly Mum's face appeared at the window, really pale and her mouth had that bitten from the inside look it gets when some disaster's happened.

Immediately, I thought of the body. I couldn't help it. What other reason would she have for disrupting the exam?

I dashed into the corridor. The only reason Mum was there was because she wanted to talk to Chris! She had to come and embarrass me. She's spoiled everything.

I've never been so furious in my life. She humiliated me in front of the whole university. Everybody saw me leaving the exam. Including Chris. God knows what *she* thought. Some stupid little Mummy's girl, running away at the first sign of trouble. I wish I'd gone to London, Edinburgh. Anywhere but Liverpool. Other people don't have to put up with their mothers butting in on crucial exams.

I couldn't go back in.

I couldn't go back home.

I couldn't go anywhere.

In the end, I spent the afternoon wandering around Sefton Park, trying to think. Everything's such a mess. I'd only done about half the paper, so there's no way I could have passed. How will I ever get the nerve to go in again?

Eventually I went round to see Chris. I knew I could rely on her. One thing about her having talked to Mum – at least she can see what I'm up against! Apparently, Mum went through the whole bit with her as well. How I was a normal girl until Chris came along. She must have talked me into it. What does she think she's playing at, taking me to London for some dirty weekend?

Chris told her she wasn't surprised I was too scared to tell her. Then she tried to calm her down, but it was no use. In a way, it's almost a good thing she saw what Mum was like. *Chris* understands me. If only Mum would . . .

We decided a weekend away was just what I need. Chris drove me back home. I ran up the stairs, grabbed my bag and left straightaway. Mum wanted to me to stay and talk. But there's no point, since she's not prepared to listen. Besides, I'm still far too angry with her.

28 June, 1994

Back home to face the music after my fantastic weekend with Chris. Mum greeted me like I'd been away for a year. She was probably worried Chris had sold me to the white slave trade.

One thing Chris had forgotten to mention – she'd let on about me and Margaret. Not that she meant to. How was she to know I'd lied to Mum?

It got really bitter. Mum went up the wall. Margaret lived with us for a while, ate our food, slept in our spare bed. I suppose it's no wonder Mum couldn't cope. It was impossible to explain that our affair happened after Margaret had moved out. I didn't get a chance to get a word in edgeways. Not that she'd 've believed me.

I tried to tell her that Margaret was my *friend*.

'So you sleep with all your friends, do you?' she shouted, really nasty.

'Friends, Family. Anyone will do.'

I couldn't help it. The words slipped out before I could stop them. I wish I hadn't said it now. Mum crumpled. She's right in a way. Dad always interferes – even when his body's buried under the patio.

I was too angry to go back on it, though. There was no way I could stay. If she'd shown me one ounce of understanding, it'd be different. I can't live there any more.

1 *July, 1994*

I feel really at home here with Chris. At first, it was like I was a guest. Once I'd unpacked and done my washing, I felt I really belonged. Officially, I'm in the spare room, but that's only where I keep my clothes!

If only it could be permanent. The day after I moved in, Chris asked me how I was going to cope with all the freedom of having my own flat. I was completely gobsmacked. Quite apart from anything else, I'm skint. No way can I afford rent till my next grant cheque comes in and that won't be until September. Basically, I need somewhere incredibly cheap. Free, in fact.

Suddenly, I had visions of me washing dishes all summer just to line the pockets of some landlord. And I'll probably have to re-sit my anatomy paper. God knows when I'll be able to revise.

Chris came to the rescue. I can stay with her for the summer. You never know. If things go well, we might decide that living together is a good thing.

Only, when I said that to Chris, she went all quiet on me. Told me I was getting ahead of myself and that it wasn't a permanent set-up. On top of that, she could even get the sack. There's people at the university who're dead jealous because she's an excellent teacher and popular. And gay. The bigots would like nothing more than to stick the knife in with half-baked accusations about her corrupting students.

I hadn't thought of that. It shouldn't matter. I'm a big girl, now. An adult. I can do what I want. Be with who I choose.

Only it *does* matter. Stupid people run the system and what they say goes.

5 July, 1994

I've failed the anatomy paper. It's official. Chris got the results before they were posted. I was totally floored. Even though I knew I wasn't going to do as well as I should. It's so humiliating – especially since I'm supposed to be going out with the lecturer.

She was no help. I asked her to fix it for me. It wouldn't have been difficult. I'd definitely have got through if I hadn't walked out. It's not like I'm incapable of passing. She's a tutor, there must have been something she could have done. A string she could have pulled.

She refused – point blank. In fact, we quarrelled about it. She said it would be totally unprofessional. Even though we've got a relationship, she's not prepared to risk her whole career on a ridiculous favour.

I never knew she could be so hard! She said I'd just have to do the same as everybody else. Re-sit in September. And ruin the whole summer, stuck indoors revising.

Everyone's against me at the moment. I went back to Brookside Close to collect the rest of my stuff. Mum collared me. If I agreed to come home, she'd graciously allow me to carry on seeing Chris and the whole thing would become a nice secret, never to be mentioned.

As if.

I'm nearly 19. I can do what I want. And I'm *not* going to crawl back home to do my revision. It's all her fault I've got to do it, in any case. I'm sick of arguing about it.

Mum went on and on. How Chris is going to get tired of me. How I'm going to get hurt. But that's the risk anyone has to take when going into a relationship. It doesn't matter whether they're male or female. Why can't she see I know exactly what I'm doing?

Then the truth came out. It's dangerous for me to get close to anyone, because of Dad. She's worried about me! Is that what it's always going to be like? Even if I met a man, she'd say the same thing. Because of what we did – because of him out there – I've got to spend the rest of my life tied to my mother's apron strings.

I'm not having that. It's emotional blackmail. No way is she going to hold *that* over me for ever and ever.

12 July, 1994

SHE DUMPED ME!
CHRIS DUMPED ME!!
Completely out of the blue. No warning at all.

Everything was going so well, too. I'd decided I wasn't going to moan about failing my anatomy paper. We were going to enjoy the summer holidays. Together. I'd made a special meal for her and everything. Spent the afternoon in the kitchen to say thank you for letting me stay.

She took one look at what I'd prepared and told me to go. Just like that. Leave by tomorrow morning. No explanation. Nothing.

It was like my entire world collapsed. How can she

be like this? When she'd said she loved me. Said she'd wanted me. What's changed? She won't tell me. All I get is stupid excuses. Like we both knew it wasn't forever. There was never any real future in it and we should never have have let it get that far.

I didn't know that. As far as I was concerned, we were a permanent item. A couple. I would have spent the rest of my life with her. She couldn't even stand me for the summer.

I was just a bit on the side for her. A notch in her bedhead. She said it wasn't like that, but how am I supposed to believe her? I bet she'd found someone else. Another naïve little student she can use whenever she feels like it.

What about Mum? Rachel? Everybody else I've upset? I left my home and family for her. I've let them all down. I just walked out and left them for Chris. I stuck up for her and trusted her. And this is how she treats me! Throws it all back in my face.

I feel so stupid. I believed everything she told me like some little schoolgirl. I can't eat. I can't sleep. Mum's been really good. After all I put her through, she just put her arms round me and let me cry on her shoulder.

IF ONLY I KNEW *WHY*.

13 July, 1994

I went round to see Chris today. I had to get her to

tell me the truth. She was packing to go away on holi-day. Our holiday. I begged her to tell me what happened. To let me know what I'd done wrong, so I could put it right.

She didn't want to tell me. Not surprising when I finally got the truth out of her. It was Mum. My own mother threatened to tell the university about us unless Chris stopped seeing me. She could have got the sack.

It wasn't worth the risk.

So now I feel a thousand times worse. Chris could've put her foot down. If she'd cared enough. She could have carried on seeing me and put two fingers up to the lot of them. Only she *didn't* care. At the end of the day, her career is the most important thing in her life – and I was just entertainment.

I've lost Mum too. How can I forgive her for what she did? I can't live there anymore. I'm never going back. I'm finished with her for good.

There was hardly anything left to pack. The only thing on my shelf was a picture of me and Mum and Rachel. Playing happy families. It was unbearable. I hurled it across the floor, smashing the frame. I spent the evening picking bits of glass out of my clothes.

23 July, 1994

Ten days of stultifying boredom!

I've spent every waking moment glued to my books. Concentrating's impossible. I keep hearing Chris's voice every time I open my notes. Apart from anything else, she's the best lecturer. Every page takes hours and hours to get into my head. My chocolate fix is up to ten bars a day! At this rate, I'll become a medical pheno- menon – the worst case of acne ever recorded! And I *still* won't be a doctor.

I miss Mum loads. It's so ridiculous, being tied to my mother's apron strings at my age. The anger won't go away. Neither will the worry. I keep having visions of her sitting in a cold, empty house. Gas cut off. Electric- ity cut off. No water. No furniture. Everything gone to pay the debts.

If only she'd made the smallest effort to understand what I'm going through. It's like I'm the only person in the world who's ever come out. I know in my head that's not true – but I *feel* like it is.

If only Chris had loved me enough to put two fingers up at the lot of them.

If only I could stop thinking about all this and get down to some work.

26 July, 1994

I went back this afternoon. Just to pick up some clothes. Mum was at work, so I didn't have to face her. In a way, I was disappointed. Like I sort of wanted her to be telepathic and know I would be round.

Rachel was in, though. Sneaking cider with Lee. They're so immature! She's doing every single boring, rebellious teenage thing she can think of. I made her promise not to tell Mum I'd been there – or I'd tell about the alcohol.

I'd just closed the front door when the house opposite

EXPLODED!!!

Suddenly the Close was full of people and glass. Our windows shattered and Rachel was inside! I dashed back and found her on the floor, covered in blood. At first, I thought she'd been knocked unconscious, but she was just stunned by the shock. You've got to hand it to her – she certainly knows how to keep her cool. Even when the ambulance arrived, she kept saying she was all right. I went to the hospital with her, leaving our local Dixon of Dock Green to get in touch with Mum.

It was so weird!! The house opposite had been squatted by a bunch of religious nutters. Fanatics. The sort who go around preying on vulnerable people, brainwashing them into believing some pathetic little toe-rag is God almighty. Literally. They make me sick. People like that are dangerous – even when they're not blowing themselves and everyone in the vicinity to kingdom come.

No doubt God told them that mass suicide was the next step in their crusade. Will they reach the kingdom of heaven? Who knows!

Rachel was all right – just cuts and bruises. We had

to wait ages for her to be seen. Then there was another age while she sat in a cubicle in a hospital gown and I sat in the corridor, waiting for Mum and thinking. I didn't have anything to distract me. Not even an anatomy book.

Supposing Rachel had been badly hurt. Or killed. Supposing Mum had been there and got caught in the crossfire. They might have died. This stupid, ridiculous – thing – might have taken them away from me. Forever.

Mum and Sinbad turned up, dead worried and upset. Luckily, Rachel showed up large as life, with only a couple of plasters on her knees as proof of her ordeal. Sinbad took her off to see how the rest of the casualties were getting on.

Seeing Mum again made me want to put all the barriers up. Part of me desperately wanted to talk to her, but I was afraid to. I couldn't face her disgust and disappointment at who I am.

'I've been worried sick,' were her first words.

There was no need. It's been one long, dreary round of revision. I haven't had time for sexual debauchery. Mum winced at that. Then she begged me to come home. Back where I belong. Regardless of who I might bring home to tea.

It was such a relief. I realized that's what I wanted – to go home. Mum can't accept me being gay, yet. She hasn't got a clue how to cope with it. She said she hadn't realized until I left that I was her best friend as well as her daughter. I suppose she's mine.

We can't make it like it was before. But that doesn't mean we can't still be best friends.

2 August, 1994

Sinbad's staying with us – tucked away in the extension! It's obvious he and Mum got a LOT closer while I was away. He's done his back in and I caught Mum putting a corset on him. And she's doing his washing.

I asked her if she'd snogged him yet, but she got all embarrassed. He's good for her. It's about time she found herself a decent man. God knows, she deserves it. But if she makes him wait too long, she might lose him . . .

The trouble is, she's scared. After everything she's been through, she's not sure if she can cope with a 'proper' relationship. The same old problem!

Mum and I are getting on much better. She wants to plan a birthday party. I can hardly believe I've managed to survive to the great age of 19! There's no-one to invite, though. All my college friends have left. Even Lucy's decided to spend the rest of the holidays back with her parents in the interests of economy.

Mike's around – and miserable! He still hasn't found a job.

I'm sick of all that love stuff. I'm obviously not very good at it. It just doesn't work. Every time, I think *this* one is going to be different, but it never is. Chris. Love just goes sour on you.

18 August, 1994

Happy Birthday to me!

Actually, it was really nice. Much better than I expected. Mum made me a waistcoat. Dead trendy AND you won't see anyone else with one like it.

The party was OK, except everyone was either over 30 or under 15. Except Mike. Still, he's a good mate. I can relax with him because he knows ALL about me. It's ironic, really. His dad is absolutely determined we should go out together. If only he knew!

Mike and I sneaked off down the pub. No-one noticed we'd gone! He's as fed up with relationships as I am. In fact, we drank a toast to celibacy. He's having an affair with his guitar. All I can say is, he needs a LOT of practice.

23 August, 1994

Typical of Brookside Close! Everyone has to know everyone else's business. Now the word going around is that Mike and I are going out together. His Dad's getting really annoying. The three of us – Mr. Dixon, Mike and I – went to get Mike's guitar. Ron spent the whole time making little digs. He's a worse wind-up merchant than Rachel. He kept on about us 'courting' – as if anyone did that anyway these days! Apparently, me and my 'fella' are a couple of love-birds.

Mike's going to have to get himself a real girlfriend,

or all these rumours about us won't stop. He says they'll stop when I meet another girl. No chance! I'm out of that market for the time being. No matter how much I fancy someone, I'm celibate. How could anyone possibly follow Chris in any case? Every day, I make up my mind not to think about her. It takes hours and hours to put her out of my mind, then I realize I've re-run the whole of our relationship in my head, yet again.

Besides, my re-sit's in a week. I'd better fall in love with my books.

30 August, 1994

It's OVER!

I went into the exam room trembling so much I could hardly hold my pen. For some reason, I thought I'd be the only one, but there were ten of us. Stupid, really. It's not as if I hadn't seen the other failures pinned up on the notice-board.

If I haven't passed this time, I'm DEFINITELY going to have the paper re-marked. It was a doddle! Easier than A Levels. Probably easier than the last one – although that's a bit hard to tell. *This* time, I didn't have my mother messing things up!

Now I've got the rest of the summer to blodge about and have a good time. I don't know who with, though. Mike's the only person around who's even remotely my age. We're going to the pictures to celebrate tonight. Should be a laugh.

28 September, 1994

I can't believe it's almost a month since I last wrote in my diary. So much for having fun! There's been nothing to write about. All I've got for today is a letter saying I've passed my re-sit.

Mum's dead pleased – and relieved. She can stop feeling guilty about ruining my last exam. I've stopped being angry with her. Even about Chris. It wasn't really Mum's fault. If she hadn't put the boot in, someone else would've. Chris didn't love me enough. End of story.

If only I didn't miss her so much.

Mike's been great. We spend our time moaning on to each other. Me about Chris. Him about being unemployed. What a wonderful summer! it must be bad – I can't wait for term to start.

5 October, 1994

First day back! Which meant only one thing – a nice, fat, juicy, grant cheque. Most of it went straight away to my bank manager. I haven't got much left after paying off my overdraft. As Sinbad put it, 'enough for a few bevvies'. A *very* few!

I'm not the only one with money problems. Mum and Sinbad were having a Council Of War round the kitchen table when I got home. Mum had her worried face on and Sinbad wasn't exactly his usual cheery self, either. It seems there's a slight cash flow problem. Another payment's due on this loan tomorrow and she's short.

EIGHTY POUNDS SHORT!

And she only missed one week. Mum wanted to ask me if I could lend her some of my grant, but Sinbad wouldn't let her. He's done a couple of odd jobs recently, so he can afford to sub her. Just as well! Having paid off one massive overdraft, I'd have to get another straight away if I had to find extra.

It's absolutely crazy. Mum's hopeless at managing her finances. All she can do is wring her hands and look helpless. God knows where the money goes. *She* certainly doesn't. Somehow, she's going to have to start looking after it. Sinbad's helped out for this week, but what about next week? And the week after that? Mum's got no idea where it's going to come from.

11 October, 1994

There's something very wrong with this stupid contract Mum signed. Why didn't she let me read it first? I'm sure she didn't go through it properly.

I bumped into her in the Parade this morning, late for work and dead worried. She's had a final demand from the HP company and one threatening legal action from the catalogue. Kenny Maguire was supposed to have paid them off. That was the point of changing over to this one big loan.

Mum got me to ring him up. She's not very confident on the phone. I tried every chance I got, at least a dozen times, and I let it ring till it went dead. No answer. Mum was almost in tears when I reported back. She's terrified he's a con man.

I told her not to panic. There's no point in worrying until we've talked to him. It may just be a mistake. Trouble is – I've a horrible feeling we've been ripped off.

In the middle of all this, Rachel swans in, demanding £3. Mum snapped at her. She hasn't got three pence, let alone three quid. As usual, Rachel's timing is perfect! She's going to have to realize this family's got money problems. Big ones!

21 October, 1994

School's broke up for half-term today. Which means a week of my grotty little sister whingeing round the house. She came home at lunchtime today, although Mum specifically told her she's to have school dinners. Lee was tagging along, as usual. According to Rach, no-one goes in on the last afternoon before half-term.

At first, Mum wouldn't let her have dinner at home. Things are tight and she can't afford it. Then Rachel produced this ten pound note. Her story was that she and Lee had been washing cars. Apparently, they made loads of money. Lee backed her up, of course, but he's not a very good liar. He goes bright red, stares hard at his shoes and just says 'yes' when Rachel tells him to.

I tackled Rachel about it when Mum went out of the room. She just opened those innocent baby brown eyes and gave me a load of flannel about washing cars. Does she honestly expect me to believe she went round every house on the estate, knocking on doors, bucket and chamois in hand? She won't even make her own bed!

She and Lee disappeared off at school time, but if they made it back to the classroom, they spent the afternoon watching the pigs flying about. They turned up again in the evening, having stuffed their faces with burgers and pizza. Some rich kid's dad treated them. Like hell.

I don't know where she's getting the money from, but if she's straight, then so is Kenny Maguire. And Ronny Biggs!

23 October, 1994

This money mess is getting worse! We've got to sort out the money management and get a proper system going. Otherwise, it's going to be loans on top of loans and we're never going to get out of it. The stupid thing is, it's so easy to get organized, but Mum can't get the hang of it.

I sat her down in the kitchen and made her go through everything systematically. Household expenditure – one column for money coming in, another for money going out. Simple. Trouble is, Mum gets all defensive. Calling me 'Miss' and saying I think she's stupid. But that's not the problem. There's nothing wrong with her brain! She just won't concentrate. As soon as we sit down to try and work out what we're going to do, she's up again to make another coffee or check the washing.

We agreed that I'd manage the money from now on. Mum has no idea how to budget. If I'm not there to watch her, she goes to the Trading Post and buys all sorts of things we don't really need. Nothing big, but little expenses add up. Like batteries, for instance. My radio went dead this morning. Mum blithely said we'd get some next time we went shopping. Only we hadn't budgeted for it. They may have been only a couple of pounds, but five extras like that, and we'd be down ten quid for the loan.

She's got to do something about Kenny Maguire. He's due round the day after tomorrow. I told her to tell him we're not happy about this loan. He's got to do what he promised – pay off the bills. At the moment, Mum's paying him every spare penny she's got, but we're no better off. In fact, it's worse. We're still getting letters from everyone and there isn't a bean to give them.

Rachel's no help. She spends enough for all of us. It's like she won't take any responsibility for being part of the family. But she's fifteen – hardly a little girl any more. Mum's delighted because she's been so quiet and well-behaved recently. Going round with her gang – all blokes, I notice. She's turning into a right little tom-boy.

There's only one thing for it – I'm going to have to find a part-time job. Trouble is, medical students have more lectures than everyone else put together. I don't want too many hours, or I'll be falling asleep in lectures. When I looked through the papers, though, even the part-time jobs mean every evening and all week-ends.

The Parade's no use either. I tried all the shops. Mike's working at the Pizza Parlour until something turns up, and his mum runs the flower-shop, but they've got all the help they need. Everyone round here's so desperate for money, every available minute is snatched up.

24 October, 1994

Kenny Maguire's been hassling Mum. You can see she's terrified of him. She just stands there, doing and undoing the middle button on her cardie, talking in such a quiet voice she's easy to ignore. And she's so polite to him! While he's patronizing the life out of her. It really does my head in.

I HATE the way he says 'Mandy'. Man-deee. All disappointed and kind. Like he's talking to a pet cat who's made a mess on the carpet.

'You can't live through these girls,' he said. 'Before

you know it, they'll be leaving home. Best not to rely on them.'

In other words, he knows he can't push me around like he can Mum.

He's just a rotten, small-time bully. As soon as I said I wanted to talk to him about the loan, he was in his car and away. Mum hadn't managed to say anything about it. He wouldn't let her get a word in. It's obvious he doesn't want us to pay him back, so he can keep collecting. The whole thing's a game – and he keeps changing the rules.

For a start, it wasn't even his day to come round. Apparently, he was dropping his new driver off. I knew Carl Banks was a toe-rag, but he's really hit rock-bottom. Working for a loan shark – how low can you get? I'd scrub toilets before I'd do anything for a man like that.

I went round to see Carl later. He *is* a neighbour and I thought maybe – just maybe – he could have a word with his boss and get him to lay off Mum. No chance! How naïve can you get!!

Carl Banks just drives. He doesn't ask questions. As far as he's concerned, Kenny Maguire only collects legitimate debts. That's how he sleeps at night – by telling himself he's only following orders. Never mind that Mum dreads Maguire coming round. Never mind all the hundreds of other people he's ripping off.

26 October, 1994

Kenny Maguire, the human leech, was back again. This time, on the right day to collect his money. I made sure I was there. Mum didn't like me missing lectures, but there was no reason why I shouldn't catch up on my notes on the kitchen table instead of at the library. Not that I did much good.

That cockroach is impossible to talk to. I asked him why we're still getting demand letters for bills he said he'd already paid off. All he'd say was 'technicalities', as if I was far too stupid to understand his financial dealings. And he called me 'sweetheart'.

I tried to get Mum not to pay. We don't have to crawl to him. We should wait until we've got concrete proof that he's keeping his side of the bargain. I'm sure what he's doing isn't right. It could even be illegal. He's just taking advantage of our problems and trying to rip us off.

Mum was useless. Worse than useless. She handed over all the money we had. Every penny. She didn't even protest. What is it with her? It's like she encourages it. First Dad, then Maguire. Men bully her and she just folds.

I lost my rag with her after he'd gone. I couldn't help it. She didn't have to let him take it. OK, so she was worried he might turn nasty, but we're not completely helpless. It was so frustrating, watching her give in like that.

I shouldn't have gone for her, though. As if she

didn't have enough to put up with. Instead of shouting back at me, she went all ashamed and quiet. Dad always used to tell her she brought it on herself because she was weak.

If he hadn't done that to her. Kept on and on and on. Making her feel pathetic and weak and stupid, she'd be able to stand up for herself now. Even though he's dead, he's still pulling her strings, dragging her down.

2 November, 1994

Pay day's come round again. Not for us – for Kenny Maguire. I really wanted to be there when he turned up, but I had a job interview this afternoon. Mum can't cope with him. Or money. She actually managed to forget a twenty pound note she had tucked into a jumper. It nearly went in with the washing! It proves my point – she's *hopeless* at managing money. We were going to put it in the tin for the loan, but there was enough there. Probably we've been scrimping and saving so much, we went a bit over the top. Which is no bad thing.

Of course, Mum's immediate reaction was to go to the shops and get us something nice for tea. The minute she gets any extra, she wants to blow it all. HOPELESS! There's no other word for it.

It's really been worrying me that she doesn't get a receipt from the Leech. What if he runs off with the money? How could she even prove she gave it to him? I made her promise a) to get a proper receipt and b) to ask him why we're still getting final demands and court summonses. We've got to have proof that these debts are being paid off. It's fatal to let bullies like Kenny Maguire intimidate you. They're all the same, his sort. You've got to stand up to them.

She promised – for all the good it did. It was un-believable! When I came home, I discovered that not only had she handed over the usual amount, he'd in-timidated her into giving him the £20 she'd found! Like he was punishing her for having the cheek to question him!

He gave her some stupid story about one of the debts having gone to the bailiffs before he bought it. As far as I'm concerned, that's his problem. The whole point of Mum signing over the debts was so she wouldn't have to pay any extra. He told Mum she could end up in prison. That can't be right. But then, there was all that stuff in the news about people being jailed for not pay-ing the Poll Tax. It would be like him to let Mum get sent down, while he disappears off with our money.

I hate it when Mum makes excuses for him. He's a businessman. He's just doing his job. Too right! His job is ripping people off.

The receipt was a farce. All he'd done was to scribble the date and amount on a scrappy piece of paper. And signed it with a dodgy signature that looks like it's been written in Cantonese.

The only good thing is that he turned up without

Carl. Apparently, Carl's got another job. His Dad gave him a real rocketing about working for a loan-shark. Seems I dropped him in it the day I went round. What a shame!

3 November, 1994

At last, I'm going to be helping out. I got the job! Max Farnham is opening a restaurant. He's gone into business with Barry Grant, of all people. How the two of them got together is anyone's guess!

The restaurant's dead classy. Max has got a bit of a thing about wine – he would have! – so the wine list is full of exotic French names at exotic French prices.

There's going to be about six waitresses. Surprise, surprise, they're all good-looking, young women. It's probably illegal under the Sex Discrimination Act, but who's going to challenge it? At least it gives me a job. The uniform's not too bad, I suppose – white blouse and short black skirt. We've got to tie our hair back and not wear too much make-up or distracting jewellery.

Opening night is 5 November. Bonfire Night. Lloyd Grossman's coming to cut a ribbon or something. Anything for a bit of publicity.

Everything's organized. The menus have been written. Invitations to the first night have been sent out.

The waiting staff are having a training session tomorrow night. The only thing we don't know is what the place is going to be called.

4 November, 1994

Rehearsal night at the restaurant. Actually, it was a real laugh. The other girls are great, especially Emma. She's very straightforward and down-to-earth. Nice-looking, too.

Barry Grant wanted us to do the silver service number. Doling out the vegetables by holding a spoon and fort like chopsticks. We tried a couple of times, but the potatoes ended up on the floor and I got green beans in the flowers. Penny Crosbie – Bing's sister-in-law – finally managed to persuade him that it wasn't the kind of thing you can learn in one evening. What an odd couple they are.

They gave us this pep talk about really wanting to make a go of the business and needing all our help and co-operation. Everything depended on us. We want to create a good impression, especially at the beginning. The usual flannel. I wish people wouldn't do that – it makes me want to squirm. What do they think we're going to do? Sabotage our jobs by telling the punters a few home truths?

5 November, 1994

I'm sick and tired of the way Kenny Maguire constantly tramples over Mum. He's supposed to come round on Wednesdays, but somehow he always seems to be in the neighbourhood.

Morning, Mandy. I'll be round in a couple of days. Good to see you.

He makes it sound so cosy and pleasant. And threatening. Like everything he says has a double meaning. Whenever he comes anywhere near me, I feel like someone's pouring a bucket of cold slime down my neck. I know what he is. I know exactly what he's doing. He's cheating us with those phony interest payments. Well, it can't go on. I'm not going to stand by and let her milk him for every penny she's got. I'm not having anyone threaten her ever again.

I decided to have it out with him. Carl told me where he'd be. The bookie's. I might have known – gambling away *our* money. And we won't see a penny of the winnings.

I was so angry I could hardly see straight. I asked him for the extra money back and proper receipts for every payment Mum's made. He was so patronizing I wanted to hit him. Calling me 'love' and 'sweetheart' and then, when I really annoyed him, 'little girl'.

The trouble is – he's got all the trump cards. That bloody agreement is completely above board. Mum signed it and he doesn't have to discuss it with anyone except her. Which suits him, because he knows she'll just do anything he tells her. As far as he's concerned, I can go to a solicitor or the police or anyone. It won't do any good.

Then he said he had more important things to be getting on with and left, leaving me standing there in the middle of the bookie's, feeling like a complete fool. More important things to do? Like playing power games with other people who aren't strong enough to stand up to him. He makes me sick.

I'll be able to help out more now I've got a job, thank goodness. It was the restaurant's first night tonight. In the end, it was a great success – but only just! Lloyd Grossman got held up. Disaster! A grand opening and no star!! Barry Grant had arranged a white stretch limo and everything. He'd even put his henchman in a chauffeur's hat. Of course, Jimmy Corkhill didn't have the sense to change out of his jeans. He looked completely ridiculous in his usual tat with this peaked cap perched on the back of his head!

Max, Patricia and Penny were going frantic, rushing round telephoning people and getting absolutely nowhere. Talk about panic. Then Barry came in and announced he'd arranged for a new celebrity. Naturally, he wouldn't let on who it is.

The moment arrived. We'd served the punters – sorry, guests – with an elegant glass of white wine and the limousine swept over the flower-beds and into the drive. (Jimmy Corkhill is *not* cut out to be a professional driver!)

Barry opened the door and out stepped

LILY SAVAGE! ! !

I thought Max Farnham was going to have a heart attack on the spot. A drag act – not quite the image he had in mind! Barry was dead cool. Introduced himself and his partner, Max. Lily Savage shook them warmly by the hand and said how wonderful it was when two men could be open about their relationship. Max's face was a picture. It kept changing colour from red to white to green, like a weird set of traffic lights. In the end he managed a pathetic little grin and choked out the words 'business partners'. The guest of honour looked dead disappointed.

Penny smiled a polite little welcome and was extra-gracious. She obviously thought all this wasn't quite the done thing. I thought Patricia was going to wet her knickers, she was laughing so much. As for David Crosbie, he was mesmerized. His eyes were literally out on stalks and he had to loosen his tie. It wasn't till later, I realized he hadn't got it! He honestly though she was a very tall woman. What an idiot! After the opening ceremony, he went to try and chat her up. I didn't hear what he said, but it was pretty obvious he soon worked out what was going on. Poor old Jean had to spend the rest of the evening calming him down. Every time I went past them, he was saying 'outrageous'.

Just as everyone had settled down to drinks and small talks, a taxi pulled up and Lloyd Grossman appeared. Seems he'd had trouble with the trains, but had battled through anyway. At least, we should get a decent write-up in the local rag.

And the name of the restaurant?

GRANTS

Just about says it all, really.

8 November, 1994

From now on, we pay Kenny Maguire what we agreed. Not a penny more. I told Mum I'd had it out with him. She was terrified. Really worried about what he might do. But he's going to have to accept we're not handing over any extra. The more we give him, the more he's going to ask for.

I made Mum promise not to let him into the house. He was supposed to come round tomorrow for the next instalment. I said I'd be there and together we'd keep him at the front door.

Only when I got back from work tonight, there he was. Sitting at our table, eating our supper. Mum had actually let him have a plate of Irish stew she'd been keeping for Sinbad.

I told him to leave. Threatened him with the police. I don't care how legitimate that contract is, it doesn't say anything about him coming into our house and invading our privacy. That's trespass. Of course, he went. His parting comment was that he hoped I wasn't going to make a habit of embarrassing him. It was a threat – but I won't be intimidated by him. If he wants a fight, he's going to get one.

Mum was no help. After all we agreed, she just let him in. He didn't need to use force. Apparently, he wanted to talk about how she's going to make the bigger repayments. What a nerve! She's gone into one of her stubborn moods now. As far as she's concerned, it's her problem so she's going to deal with it. Badly.

19 November, 1994

Barry Grant's latest promotional idea is a nightmare! He's produced these skimpy new uniforms for the waitresses. Tiny little black dresses with straps so thin you can't wear a bra and a skirt so short it barely covers your bum. We could get done for indecent exposure wearing them in public. It's really demeaning. All the old letch businessmen are constantly dropping their forks to make us bend down. One bearded creep kept putting his arm round Emma's waist while he was ordering.

Management was no help. Penny told us to smile and back off gracefully. As for Barry . . . Think of the uniform as 'nouvelle cuisine', he said. There isn't much of it, but what there is looks really good.

When I said I'd slap the next one that tried it on, he threatened to give me my P45. Pointed out that there's plenty of other girls out there, unemployed, who'd be glad of the job. Basically, he's blackmailing us. It's appalling that we should have to put up with sexual harassment at work. Trouble is, he's right.

The final straw was when Kenny Maguire turned up. He was delighted to see me serving him. Really pandered to his ego. He was practically dribbling into the soup. Then he had the nerve to pat my bum.

No way was I standing for that!

Emma and I gave him a groper special. I poured him a glass of rich, fruity red wine. 'Oh dear, what a shame! Emma's bumped into me and the wine's gone all over your expensive suit. So sorry, sir. Let me get you a cloth so I can spread the stain a little bit further.'

We'd had enough, though. Tomorrow, our uniforms are going to be in the wash. Permanently.

20 November, 1994

Penny's on our side! In a roundabout, discreet sort of way. Emma and I went back to the old uniforms. When we said the new ones were being washed, she just said she thought they might be.

Barry was furious. He wasn't going to let us get away with it. No uniform, no job. Emma was brilliant. She said he couldn't sack us, because we were going to strike. Just like that! So now we've officially withdrawn our labour. The other girls downed cutlery and we marched out. Penny, Max and Barry had to serve out Sunday lunch themselves.

They're going to have to manage dinner as well. And every other meal from now on. Tomorrow, we're going to have a proper picket line outside the restaurant. The idea is to stop the staff and customers from crossing it. There's no way all those businessmen are going to put up with the hassle. They'll just go somewhere else.

Barry Grant hasn't got a hope in hell.

21 November, 1994

Up the workers! United we stand!
WE'VE WON!!!
It was brilliant. The six of us spent the day outside the restaurant telling customers what we were doing and why. Most of them couldn't care less about the cause, but they went away anyway. Probably lost their custom for good.

David Crosbie turned up. He's got a vested interest, since Max Farnham is his son-in-law. Honestly, he's such a hypocrite. He went on and on about young people today, wanting more money and longer holidays without even bothering to listen to what we were saying. When we finally got through to him that we were protesting about being forced to wear degrading uniforms, he called me an anarchist and said we should be proud to wear them. King and Country and all that rubbish. I bet if he actually saw what Barry wanted us to wear, he'd be bursting a blood vessel at the sight of that wicked flesh.

The next thing that happened was that Jimmy Corkhill turned up with Mo, the barmaid from La Luz.
Jimmy Corkhill was totally obnoxious as usual, but Mo
said we had a legitimate grievance. Joined the picket
line there and then. It was great. We all started shouting slogans.

SUPPORT THE STRIKE
STOP SEXPLOITATION IN THE WORKPLACE

Mo threatened to bite the legs off anyone who
crossed our picket line. Only three people actually had
lunch. And they were in and out in half an hour – not
much profit there. About half past three, Barry, Max
and Penny came out. They agreed to forget about the
new uniforms if we'd agree to work on Christmas Day.
Emma got them to pay double time and a half for it. For
that money, I'd've done it anyway. So would the
others.

Power to the people.

25 November, 1994

Why won't Mum tell me what's going on? Why
won't she let me help? I keep catching her in floods of
tears. She says it's this debt business and Rachel hassling her all the time for material possessions so she can
keep up with her little friends. But there's more to it

than that. That creep Maguire's got some sort of hold over her.

Last Wednesday, I found the two of them together. Mum looked like a ghost. He was drinking tea, making himself at home. No way I was letting him drink it. On the way out, he turned to Mum.

'Remember what I said, Mandy,' he said. 'Think about it.'

Mum won't tell me what he was going on about. Made up some story about a new repayment plan. Lower payments and higher interest, probably. It didn't ring true, though.

This morning was the worst. The doorbell rang and there were these two thugs at the door. As soon as Mum opened it, they barged in, pushed a piece of paper into her hands, grabbed the sewing machine and charged out again.

Bailiffs. The piece of paper was a warrant from the court! The sewing machine payments haven't been paid for months!! God knows what we're going to do. Mum can't even earn any extra money from her sewing any more. We can't live on her wages from cleaning the school. She gets a pittance! We'll get more and more behind.

How much more proof does Mum need to see that Kenny Maguire's ripping us off? I got her to admit how much she owed him. £3,000. Three thousand pounds. I hadn't a clue it was such a lot. She's found out about my overdraft – £1,800. At least I got the money from a bank – not some stupid loan-shark.

We've got to do something. I'm frightened even to answer the door. It's about time I started to pull my weight around here, instead of leaving Mum to scrape by for the three of us. I've got to earn some extra money. Barry and Max'll take me on full-time at the restaurant. And I'll have to take a year out from university. I can finish my course any time. There's no other way out of this mess.

28 November, 1994

It's all organized. I went to see my tutor this afternoon. He was really good about it. Told me I've got more than sufficient grounds to defer for up to a year. I don't have to confirm anything till after Christmas, but I've made up my mind now. What other option is there? Barry Grant was fine. I explained the situation to him and he said he'd be really pleased for me to go full time.

That's it. Sorted. We're going to be OK over Christmas. And every Christmas from now on.

So why do I feel so depressed? It's only for a year. I can go back to my course, pick up where I left off. Loads of people do it, I'm hardly over the hill. In fact, I'm younger than a lot in my year. I *will* go back. I promise myself.

I WILL GO BACK

The trouble is, supposing I can't? Supposing this horrible business doesn't sort itself out? I could be stuck peeling spuds at Barry Grant's caff for the rest of my life.

Mum went up the wall when I told her. Screaming and smashing plates on the floor. It was awful! She went on and on about how I shouldn't waste what's in my head. How I should leave the waiting on and the washing up to the likes of her.

The numbskulls!

That's what she called herself. A numbskull. Why does she always put herself down? If only I could give her a bit of confidence. And this isn't helping – she's gone on a complete guilt trip. She told me she's not having it, but what choice have we got? Unless she can come up with a better idea, this is the way it's going to have to be.

30 November, 1994

A miracle's happened. We're off the hook. All of us! I still can't quite believe it's happened.

Mum's actually pulled it off. She came in this evening beaming all over her face. Apparently, she decided to go for a walk to clear her head – she'd had a migraine all day. After wandering around for hours, she decided to get a cup of tea in the local bingo hall. Someone won £500, so she blew our last fiver on a game. Got a full house first go.

It was as easy as that. She won three thousand pounds. Exactly what we owe Kenny Maguire. She got them to make the cheque out to him and went straight round to give it to him.

He's out of our lives forever. We don't owe anyone a bean.

It's unreal. All these months of worrying – and it's over. I can't quite take it in. Mum went to get her hair done and Sinbad and I got a Chinese takeaway. We ate in stunned silence. Do things like this really happen?

6 December, 1994

WHAT IS GOING ON?
The bailiffs shoved their way back in again. This time, they were after the TV. More payments missed. Another county court judgement. Mum told Rachel it'd gone for repair and now she's complaining about missing her daily fix of Australian soaps.

We're not out of the woods yet. Even though Mum won the bingo and everything, it doesn't mean we can take things easy. We still haven't got enough money to manage properly. I caught her today dressed up to the nines, about to go and snap up every seasonal rip off in town. I told her I don't want anything for Christmas and I'm going to have a word with Rachel as well. Until I know our finances are under control, Christmas is off!

I can't get a straight answer out of Mum. She's supposed to have written about the TV. It'll take ages to sort out. Then there's the other bills. Are they paid off? It's a perfectly simple question, but Mum manages to avoid it every time.

Maguire was round here again. Not to take money this time – to lend us a TV. I don't get it. What's in it for him? Why does he keep coming round when he's been paid off? Mum said he was just being considerate. That's rubbish! He's a complete creep.

She couldn't possibly fancy him. Could she?

The atmosphere at home's unbearable, so I went to see Mike. Sometimes I think he's the only thing that's keeping me sane! His sister's just got a flat on the Parade, so we went round there to hang out. Jacqui and her mate, Katie Rogers, are typical teenagers. Just left school. First job. First flat. First taste of independence. It's quite sweet, watching them play house. I suppose I'm a bit jealous.

They're not much younger than me and Mike, but they seem generations away. Like I've lived a thousand years more than them, but on the other hand, I can't get away from home. There's no way I can leave Mum yet. I'd love to be independent. Have a place of my own. Mike actually asked me if I'd share with him. Once he's found a job!

It would be great! He's so easy going and friendly. *And* he knows all about me, so there wouldn't be any hassle about bringing women home or him fancying me or anything. We'd have to have a few ground rules. Like no pinching each other's girlfriends!

Jacqui and Katie are convinced we're seeing each other. We've both told them we're just mates, but they don't believe it. Saying we might be sharing a flat doesn't help! I don't care what other people think, as long as we know the truth.

It was a brilliant evening. Mike got out his wonderful new guitar and we harmonized 'Silent Night' until the guy from the Pizza Parlour came up to complain. I didn't think we were that bad! Later on, we switched the lights out and told ghost stories by candlelight. The shadows from the Christmas tree made the room dead spooky.

Mike went over the top, though. He's a good storyteller, but one of them really freaked me out. Because it's true. Three years ago, a woman and her kid were murdered. Pushed off the scaffolding. The bloke that did it was killed himself.

'Makes you wonder,' he said. 'What happens to all these people who go missing. There's probably bodies buried all over the country and nobody'll ever know about it.'

It was like he'd walked over the patio and trodden on the body down there. Suddenly, the whole business re-played in my head. That tramp Mum said was Dad. He was somebody's son. Somebody's brother. Father, maybe. One day, he left and never came back. There are people out there still waiting for him. They'll never know he's been decently buried. That there's a gravestone at his head – labelled TREVOR JORDACHE.

All this stupid talk did my head in. I really didn't

fancy walking back through the alley. Even with Mike holding my hand. Jacqui said I could stay the night. Mike stayed too. He and I cuddled up under the same duvet. I know Jacqui's dead suspicious, but it's no problem. *We* both know each other's situation. It's not as if he fancies me or anything.

7 December, 1994

I came home to find all hell breaking loose. Rachel's only been caught shoplifting. She and Lee were caught with a couple of their so-called mates in the precinct in town. It's been going on for weeks! A proper, organized little gang. The little bitch! I could cheerfully strangle her for this. What the hell did she think she was playing at?

Mum had disappeared. I'm convinced she keeps out of the way every Wednesday in case Maguire shows up. Rosie Banks came round and told me what happened. She'd talked to the police, who said they'll just give them a caution some time next week. None of the kids know, so we decided to keep them sweating for a bit. Teach them a lesson.

Then she dropped the bombshell. The shop will only agree not to prosecute if they can have the stolen goods back. And guess where my brilliant little sister hid them? Under the patio.

There was nothing I could do. The police were already on their way over with shovels and spades.

Rachel showed them where to dig. I've never been so scared in all my life, watching them take up the flag stones one by one. If she'd gone one more to the right, they'd have found the body.

I was concentrating so hard, I didn't notice Mum come back. She burst through the kitchen door just as they hauled up a black bin bag. The same kind we used. She was completely hysterical, paralysed.

'I'm sorry. I didn't mean it. I'm sorry. I didn't mean it.'

Over and over again, until she collapsed. Slid down the wall in a heap like someone had bashed her on the back of the head. I managed to catch her and tell her really loud and strong what was going on. Luckily, no-one else heard her exact words. Under the circumstances, it wasn't surprising she went off her rocker.

Everyone went away after that. Rachel and Mum had a right slanging match. Trouble is, we all know why she did it. Sick of being called a 'pov' in school. OK, so she gets teased a bit. She ought to have more sense. And more consideration. The last thing Mum needs right now is this.

15 December, 1994

Christmas is coming – and it's going to be a good one!

I met Sinbad on the Parade hidden under a

mountain of paper. Someone's going to get a lot of pressies. Or one big one. One very big one. In fact, a present the size of a house.

A house with a number 10 on it – and not the one in Downing Street either.

Sinbad's bought our house. His Mum sold hers when she moved to Australia and gave him £45,000. Forty. Five. Thousand. POUNDS. He's been planning it for ages. It's all arranged, deposit, mortgage, the lot.

Mum's going to be absolutely thrilled when she finds out. She's gone shopping, so the coast's clear for him to get cracking on the house. I lent him my keys so he could lay on a bit of a spread for her as well. Talk about chuffed. I've never seen our window-cleaner so happy. I asked him if he was going to move in with us, but at the moment, he's planning to be an absentee landlord. Not too absent, I hope . . .

Mike was in a good mood, too. Seems he already knew Sinbad's so-called secret. Mum's going to be the last to hear about it. Anyway, I thought it would be good idea if I kept out of the way. Left Mum alone with Sinbad to say thank you. You never know what might happen.

It was absolutely imperative that we celebrate, so we decided to hold a party round at Jacqui and Katie's. Creepy Carl muscled in, but I was far too happy to object. The plan of action is to go round all the halls of residence and student houses to drum up support. Bring bottle and party hat. Then it's off to Sainsbury's for the booze. Finally, all we need to do is to persuade Jacqui and Katie that it's a good idea.

16 December, 1994

Rachel's gone missing. She and Lee were supposed to face the music at the police station yesterday afternoon, but they didn't show up. It's so typical! She's completely irresponsible. Never thinks of how Mum might feel. How worried she'd be.

Mum came to find me at the party this morning, completely frantic. In her lurid imagination, Rachel's already been abducted to join the white slave trade. It's much more likely she's hiding out somewhere. Mum and Sinbad have tried all her mates, but she won't have gone far. Not just before Christmas.

Mike was a real hero. Even Carl showed his good side. They spent the afternoon hanging around town, checking out the shops. In his own, quiet way, Mike's a genuinely kind person. Just because he isn't always shouting his mouth off or trying to be witty, people think he's a wimp. He's been a good friend to me, which is far more important.

Of course, Mum's busy getting the wrong idea about us – even while she's worried sick about Rachel. I'd stayed over at the party and slept next to Mike. When Mum rang the doorbell, I was still wearing Mike's T-shirt – I hadn't brought anything of my own to sleep in. Then, Mike came out in his boxers.

Mum looked gobsmacked. Half-pleased that I might be turning 'normal' or that my 'gay phase' is over. Half-shocked that I could be having sex. I told her there was nothing in it, that we're just mates. I haven't suddenly turned straight.

She wanted to know how a Lesbian could do that. It's so simple! Because we're friends – and friends do that kind of thing. Could this be the good ol' generation gap? All these rigid rules – the only possible contact you can have with a member of the opposite sex is to sleep with them. And the only possible contact you can have with your own is to be purely platonic friends. Sometimes, I think she'll *never* understand.

17 December, 1994

No news.

The whole neighbourhood's been out searching. The police are out after them. Nothing. I reckon they've probably hitched to London. Rachel's stupid enough to do that – and Lee does whatever she tells him.

Rachel's taken everything with her. Clothes, washing stuff, make-up. I got this awful sick feeling at the bottom of my stomach when I saw how little was left. I couldn't kid myself it was a spur of the moment thing. She planned it. Really planned to go away. For good.

Mum's going crazy. Like something's snapped inside her. She got it into her head that Rachel left some clue in her bedroom. A letter from someone or an article about a place or something. I dunno. Neither did Mum. Just something. Anything.

Mum spent the whole morning in there, searching

through what was left. Sinbad and I just watched from the door. He was clinging to the frame as though we were on a dinghy in a storm, getting more and more anxious. Mum chucked all the old junk from the back of the drawers on to the floor. Piles of Just 17s stacked under the bed were dragged out and torn up. Then she started on the furniture, swinging the drawers on the floor so hard I could hear the wood splintering as it knocked the bed frame.

All the time Mum was muttering under her breath. 'There must be a clue here. There's got to be.'

She got louder and louder until she was screaming at the top of her voice. I couldn't bear it – seeing her out of control. Literally out of her mind with worry.

It was unbearable. I had to get her to stop. She wouldn't listen. Couldn't listen. My hand came up and slapped her round the face. I hit my own mother!

The world stopped. Suddenly, everything went quiet. Mum didn't say a word. Just stared at me, completely blank, like she couldn't remember where she was. Then she crumpled up and cried. Sinbad put his arms round her and they rocked together.

Poor Mum. She feels so useless. Her daughter's out there somewhere, but all she can do is wait. It's the most positive thing, really. Someone's got to be here in case the police call back.

18 December, 1994

No news.

I spent the day going round Rachel's friends. Mike was in town again. Nothing. Her so-called mates are so bloody smug! Like Rachel's done this wonderful, brave thing. Never mind what could happen to her.

She's just a stupid, irresponsible, thoughtless, insensitive KID, who doesn't know what the hell she's doing. I'll kill her when she comes back.

If she comes back.

19 December, 1994

No news.

20 December, 1994

No news.

21 December, 1994

No news.

Kenny Maguire's been sniffing round here again. He's always hanging around. Now that Mum's paid him off, he wondered if she wanted a new loan. To pay for

Christmas presents. Oh, and he's got a posh new office. Paid for with *our* money.

Our friendly, neighbourhood loan-shark was dead sympathetic about Rachel. He told Mum he'd use his contacts to put the word out. Mum can't see he's just saying that. All he wants is for her to be in debt to him again.

She didn't agree to the new loan, but I'm worried that she might be conned by him again. Why, after all she's been through, is she so trusting?

There's a Medics Ball coming up at uni on 5 January. Just as we've all got over our New Year's Eve hangovers, it's time to get completely sloshed again! I asked Mike to come with me, seeing as there's no romance for me on the horizon. All we've got to do now is learn to dance! It's going to be the real thing – suits, posh frocks and lots of left-footed medical students trying to waltz.

We practised round at Jacqui's. Carl came along to criticize. He practically cheered when me and Mike collapsed on to the sofa. We're hopeless!

It was brilliant fun – then I suddenly got this vision of Rachel. Like I could see her standing all by herself in the rain down some disgusting dark alley. What was I doing enjoying myself, when she could be starving or raped or murdered? I should have been out there, looking for her. The last thing I should be thinking of is dancing.

22 December, 1994

Lee's back. I don't know if it makes things better or worse.

Better – because we know that up to yesterday, at least, Rachel was alright. And we've got some idea where she is.

Worse – because she's completely on her own now.

Apparently, they hitched to London. (Hitched! Two fifteen-year-olds! I thought Mum was going to faint when she heard. I thought I would.) They found themselves a grotty B & B, saw the bright lights and promptly ran out of money. Rachel said they ought to shoplift for a living. Lee said they ought to go home. They ended up quarrelling outside *Les Miserables*.

Lee left her there. Said he was going to hitch back to Liverpool and dumped her in the middle of London. Got home this afternoon to be treated as the Prodigal Son by Rosie and Eddie.

As for Rachel. . . . She sent a message via Lee.

TELL MUM I'M ALRIGHT AND NOT TO WORRY.

So, of course, we all start panicking. In a way, though, it was a relief. At least we can *do* something. Sinbad decided to go straight down to London. David Crosbie, of all people, said he'd go with him. He was really organized. Arranged for us to find recent photos, gave Lee the third degree on where he'd last seen Rachel. I never thought I'd be grateful for his Brookside Residents Association.

Mum and I went through every frame and album and drawer in the house. We found a couple of good snaps and it kept our minds off what might be happening to Rachel for a couple of hours.

I had to keep telling Mum over and over again that Rachel would be alright. But the more I said it, the less I believed it. She's never been to London in her life. How's she going to cope on her own? Why on earth did Lee leave her like that?

I went round to see Mike. As soon as I was away from Mum, it was like all my defences collapsed. I ended up in floods of tears, crying on Mike's shoulder. I can't remember when I've felt so worried. He cuddled me until I felt a bit better.

He wanted me to stay, but I couldn't bear to be away from Mum any longer. Kenny Maguire's car drove off as I got home. Over supper, I asked her what he wanted. Seems he came to ask after Rachel. Very friendly – I don't think! Mum's falling for it. Says he's not that bad. Just because he offers a few words of sympathy, she thinks he's suddenly become a human being.

She won't eat. She stares at her plate as though the food's going to leap up and choke her.

23 December, 1994

If I see another Santa Claus collecting money, I'm going to scream. I can't stand the fairy lights and decorations. Everyone's celebrating except us. I keep telling myself Rachel will come home for Christmas, but it's almost here and there's no news.

Sinbad rang in to say he and Mr. Crosbie have found a guest-house. No sign of Rachel, though. They've been going round the kids on the streets. The homeless ones. Runaways without even a roof over their heads. Junkies. Underage prostitutes. Kids who simply disappear.

Out there – somewhere – is my little sister. If she hasn't already been swallowed up by the city.

I couldn't keep still. It's awful not being able to do anything, so I went to find Kenny Maguire. I had to know why he's still pestering her when she's paid him off. He acted so innocent. Surprised to see me. He'd only popped in to see if we'd heard from Rachel.

But what about the other times? He's never away. He had the cheek to say he'd got quite fond of Mum. That they had more than a 'borrower/lender' relationship.

What the hell did he mean by that? They can't be seeing each other, surely? He must be lying! Supposing he's not, though. If he's not coming round to collect money and Mum's not getting another loan, what else could it be? How could she go out with a creep like that?

24 December, 1994

I had to find out what was going on. If Maguire wouldn't tell me, there was only one thing for it –

tackle Mum. In a way, I was hoping she'd say he was intimidating her or that he'd forced her to take out a new loan. Anything, rather than face the fact that my mother wants to go out with a scuzzy loan-shark.

He's considerate. A friend. Sort of. What the hell does 'sort of' mean? She must be seeing him. There's no other explanation. In the end, she told me to leave her alone.

She hasn't said a word to me all morning.

Later

Rachel's back! She crept in the back door, like she was a bit late back from school. No explanations. Nothing.

Once she got over the relief, Mum was furious. Who can blame her? Rachel hasn't a clue what she put Mum through, what with the police and everything. Anything could have happened to her. All she could say was 'it's alright, I'm back now'. The more Mum yelled at her, the more she sulked.

There was nothing I could do. Only stand back and let the two of them fight it out. Eventually, Mum couldn't stand it any longer. She hit Rachel. Slapped her round the race really hard. I put my arms round her, but she didn't need protecting. Mum collapsed into tears as soon as she'd done it. The whole thing was a reaction to the days and days of worry.

What is it with this family? As soon as there's the tiniest problem, we turn to violence.

26 December, 1994

What a way to spend Christmas Day! I couldn't believe so many people could possibly want to spend the most family-oriented day of the year at a restaurant. Actually, it was incredibly good fun. Instead of people coming in at all times and ordering stuff from the menus, we made the whole event into a party.

The dinner itself was roast goose with the most amazing trimmings I've ever seen. Three sorts of stuffing, little round roast potatoes, vegetables presented in little kidney dishes and matched for colour. And it tasted nice!

I've never been so hungry in my life. Of course, the staff didn't have a minute to grab a mouthful. After lunch, Barry made sure all the staff had a food parcel to take home. I can never decide about him. One moment, he's dead nice and generous, the next he's playing the hard man.

One thing's for sure – there's something going on between him and Emma. They never stop needling one another. Pity, in a way. She's quite fanciable. Anyway, she's coming to the Medics Ball with me and Mike. Take her mind off Barry Grant. Mike and I are going to fix her up with someone. I told her we'd be able to, but now I can't think of a single person.

Home was much better. It was probably just as well I was out of the way for a bit. When I got back, Mum and Rachel were much more relaxed. Rachel still hasn't let on what she did by herself in London. How she survived. In a way, I'm quite proud of her. She and Mum were both very quiet. It was a bit sticky at first, but they've kind of made it up. I discussed it with Mum, and we both agreed we'd wait for Rachel to tell us what happened. Maybe nothing did. Maybe she just missed us all and decided to come home, but I have a feeling there's more to it than that.

We had an amnesty over Christmas. Forgot all our problems, pulled crackers, watched the telly and demolished the remains of Grants' smoked salmon.

Mike came over this afternoon with a Christmas presi. A camisole, no less. Cream silk with roses. Very sexy! Mum was dead suspicious. Probably because she'd love us to be more than just good friends.

Sinbad hasn't been near the place. There was nothing under the tree from him. I thought he'd've at least called round for a mince pie or something. I really missed him. One thing's for sure – he and Mum have quarrelled. And I can guess what about! A certain over friendly loan shark.

I asked Mum, but she denied it. She said she couldn't stand the way he charged in here and bought the house up without even telling her. The more she says it's got nothing to do with Maguire, the less I believe her.

Why won't she admit it? The truth is she's having an affair with Kenny Maguire and Sinbad found out about it. It's the only logical explanation. Actually, I *do* know why. Because I can't stand the idea of her going with that creep. On the other hand, if she likes him . . .

She says he's considerate. He did lend us a telly and asked after Rachel. Who knows? Maybe he even made a few phone calls. He isn't exactly my idea of the ideal man, but he must have a few good points.

Besides, the guy virtually told me as much himself. More than a 'borrower/lender relationship'. At the time, I thought he was boasting. Now, I'm not so sure.

27 December, 1994

A few good points! Kenny Maguire!!

I should trust my instincts. The man is a slimeball, a rat, the lowest of the low.

I told Mum what he'd said. Finally, she admitted what's been going on. She's not having an affair with him. She slept with him because he said he'd clear her debts. That's how my mother pays the bills! There was no bingo win. It was all a big lie. I should have known. Nothing's that easy!

Only it wasn't just the one time. Now he won't leave her alone. Every month, she has to pay the next instalment. In kind.

That's what Sinbad found out. That's why he hasn't been round. He can't face her! I'm not sure that I can. How could she? How could she sleep with someone and just let them use her like that?

Then she had the nerve to get angry with Sinbad, because he left it so long before telling her he had the money. It's not his fault. Where does all this leave them? At long last, Mum realizes that Maguire's conned her. Made her look a complete fool. Probably lost her the only real chance of happiness she's ever had.

And the debt's still aren't cleared.

28 December, 1994

I haven't been able to think about anything else. Sleep was completely impossible. I wish I hadn't been so hard on Mum. A lot of the things she said made sense, once I got over being angry.

She saw seeing her children go without Christmas presents. Saw me nearly throwing my education away to work full-time as a spud-peeler instead of becoming a doctor. I think I understand now. She did it for me and for Rachel. She just switched herself off and said, 'Right, you can have what you want, but then leave me and my family alone'.

Only of course he didn't.

Mum never considers herself. Never thinks *she* might be worth something. It's the story of her life. All those times she went with my dad after he'd battered her. After what he did to me. It was the only way she knew how to protect us. Sex had nothing to do with it – the point was to survive.

29 December, 1994

Somehow, I've got to get Sinbad and Mum back together. They love each other. Real, proper, true love. What they've got is far too good to waste. It blows my dad and Kenny bloody Maguire right out of the water.

I bought Sinbad some aftershave, but I didn't get a chance to give it to him. Mum was going to the shops, so I tried to persuade her to hand it over. She just smiled this sad little smile. Nice try!

He's dead cut up about it. I found him on the Parade this afternoon. After all that's happened, this is really ripping his heart out. I could really see things from his point of view. It took him eighteen months to build up to a kiss. Then, Kenny Maguire comes along, clicks his fingers and Mum jumps into bed with him.

He said he still loves her, but how's he supposed to cope with being rejected like that? We talked for hours, sitting on that bench, freezing to death and avoiding the bird's mess.

What he really wants to do is to shove that three grand right down Maguire's throat. He can actually afford it – there's still a bit left even after buying the house. Only he was worried what Mum would say. Not surprising after all the grief she gave him about surprising her with the house.

Still, it's his money and it'd get Maguire off Mum's back once and for all. What can she say to that? So he's going to go for it.

30 December, 1994

What is it with Kenny Maguire? Sinbad took the £3,000 round and he turned it down! I knew the man was into power games, but this is unbelievable. He can't let go of his victim. Not even when there's filthy lucre being waved under his nose.

Sinbad came into the kitchen with his mouth bleeding. When Maguire wouldn't take the money, Sinbad swung at him. Poor old Sinbad! He's no Frank Bruno. Maguire slammed his face on the desk, bust his face and told him to get out. The only person who can pay back the money is Mum. His victim!

So Sinbad tries to give the money to Mum. Will she take it? No! She's gone all stubborn again. Wants to sort the problem out herself. Never mind that a) Sinbad really loves her, b) she really loves him and c) he can afford it. Honestly, I wanted to shake her. She makes me so mad. Why won't she give her stupid pride a rest?

Finally, Sinbad persuaded her. They made it up and she went round to pay over the money. Fine, says Maguire. Pay the £3,000. Oh and what about the early repayment clause! Didn't you read the small print? Didn't you have a microscope on you when you signed? If she pays early, she has to find another 33% on top of everything else. An extra thousand pounds.

She took back the money and came home. What else could she do? How are we ever going to get out of this mess?

1 January, 1995

New Year's Resolution – don't get drunk!

I had an excellent time, though. A gang of us managed to do three clubs before midnight. We were going on to a new place in town to see the New Year in, when I suddenly got homesick. After everything that's happened, I just wanted to be with my family.

They – Sinbad included – were round at the Banks. Rose and Eddie are real party animals underneath their suburban exteriors! I got there at exactly midnight.

Mike was there, though, standing around like a spare part, so I had to give him a new year kiss! I hadn't really had a chance to thank him for the Crimbo present, anyway.

1995 can't possibly be as traumatic as 1994.

2 January, 1995

Once I'd got over my hangover, it was time to pay some serious attention to THE MEDICS BALL. Of course, I didn't have anything suitable to wear, so I went into town to see what there was in the sales. Things may have been reduced, but even half-price, they were still way beyond my means. Eventually, I found this long black strappy number for a tenner. What I'd do without Oxfam, I don't know.

The next problem was how to get round proper ballroom dancing. I don't know my quickstep from my tango. However, it seems there are some secret ball-room fiends on the Close. David Crosbie, of all people, is apparently a whizz-kid waltzer. He used to dance with Julia Brogan in competitions and all sorts. I tend to steer clear of her a bit, ever since she roped me into playing at last year's Carol Concert for the OAPs. She's a right old busybody. Still, she offered to take me in hand and Mr. Crosbie volunteered to give Mike a few hints.

Julia came round here and Mike went across to Bing's. It was actually going quite well. I could get into this dancing lark. Emma came round in a bit of a gloom. She's quarrelled with Barry. Again.

I felt embarrassed. The only person Mike could think of to invite to the ball is already going with someone else, so it looked like Emma was going to be playing gooseberry. Although it did cross my mind to get her and Mike together!

The girls joined the boys chez Crosbie. We caught Mike dancing with Carl! Two lads together – looking quite fetching. Of course, they leapt to opposite sides of the room when we came in. It was dead funny. Julia and Mr. Crosbie were practically having a stand-up fight to see who'd got the better pupil. Mike's got two left feet, but then, I've probably got two right ones, so we should be OK.

We solved the problem of Emma's partner – sort of. Carl's coming with us. Emma didn't look exactly chuffed, but it was the best we could come up with. Pity he can't dance, though. Emma's had lessons and everything. I had a bit of a go with her and she's really good.

Sinbad's being amazing. When I showed him my dress, he insisted on giving me £40 for another one. Not because he didn't like Oxfam's best, but he didn't want me going to my first big dance in second-hand gear. It's typical of him to be so thoughtful. I was quite choked. As far as I'm concerned, he's definitely part of the family.

3 January, 1995

I bought myself the most glamorous, elegant dress imaginable. Long, black and strappy and it fits like a glove. It's quite like the Oxfam one in style, but it looks a thousand times better. There's something about wearing brand new clothes that does it for me. As soon as I tried it on, I started to get excited about the dance.

I'm definitely putting the past behind me. For the first time in ages, I found myself thinking about Chris today. It doesn't hurt nearly so much now. I suppose I still miss her. A bit. And it would be nice to have a real partner to go to the dance with, instead of just Mike. But the whole thing was a big mistake.

I showed Sinbad my new dress and he loved it. I can't get over him being so generous. But it's embarrassing, living on handouts. Maguire only makes things worse.

When I said that to Sinbad, he got all mysterious.

He's sorted someone out to deal with that bloody leech once and for all. That's all the information I could get out of him! With any luck, Maguire's going to be out of the picture soon. He wouldn't let on who he'd got lined up or how they're going to do it. I only hope he's not going to get himself into trouble.

5 January, 1995

Actually, it's the 6th. I can't sleep, so I thought I'd write down what happened tonight.

The ball was excellent. Mike looked good, in dinner jacket and black tie. Carl, as usual, was being a right prat. Instead of a proper shirt, he had T-shirt with a dickey bow printed on it. What a divvie! Emma was furious. She was dressed up to the nines. Really smart.

He couldn't dance to save his life. Emma tried to get him to keep time, at least, but it was completely hopeless. We had a good laugh at them. That Carl doesn't half fancy himself. According to Mike, he's under the impression he's well in with Emma. As if! She's got a lot a lot more taste than that.

Mike and I made quite good partners, dancing together. It was a bit precarious to start with, but we started to get the hang of it after a while. Loads of people were beginners, so it didn't matter that we weren't exactly professional. At one point, Emma kindly pointed out that I was the one leading.

Personally, I can't see why that's a problem. Equality in relationships – that's what I say.

We were having a bit of a rest at our table, when this girl came up, selling tickets to a 'Sumo wrestling competition'. Carl 'I'm so hunky' Banks was easy prey. He had to get up in this enormous pink plastic thing and bounce off another victim. Looking like a prize idiot suits him!

The girl was nice, with cute blonde plaits, like a little Heidi. She said we'd met, but I couldn't remember her. I suppose I was kind of keeping an eye out for her the rest of the evening. We found each other at the bar and introduced ourselves properly. Viv's a trainee lab technician – and she drinks in the same bar as Chris and I used to!!! That's how come she recognized me. She'd even been out with Chris.

So much for me being the one and only. I might have known. All the nice girls love a lecturer.

As Mike and I were leaving, Viv gave me a scrap of paper with her phone number on it. I'd really like to ring her, but I'm not sure I should. I *did* say I was going to be celibate from now on. On the other hand, she's my own age and dead attractive and looks like she'd be a lot of fun. Could be just what I need!

Mike got all confidential on the way back. His family's a right mess – and I thought ours was bad. His Dad's gone off with a woman half his age. That wouldn't be too bad, only this Bev also had a one-night stand with Mike. She then gets pregnant, and guess who turns out to be the baby's father? Mike! He said it's doing his head in. Saddled with a kid when he's only just graduated.

When we got back to the Close, Mike wanted to talk some more. As if all this baby nonsense wasn't enough, he's in love. He kept that one quiet! Just as he was about to reveal the name of his beloved, Sinbad emerged out of the shadows.

Whatever Sinbad had lined up for Kenny Maguire has fallen through. No-one'll help him. Not even Barry Grant, who's usually willing to damage anyone for a friend. Now Sinbad's threatening to go after Maguire himself, to pay him back for what he did to Mum.

I told him I'd come with him, but he refused. His excuse was that I might get hurt.

Me? What if something happens to *him*? He's hardly Mr. Universe. Maybe once he's slept on it, he'll calm down and see sense. Maguire's much bigger than him. He could do Sinbad some serious damage. That scumbag wouldn't think twice about it.

But if he doesn't come to his senses, there's only one thing for it. I'm not going to let Sinbad out of my sight. If he goes for Maguire, I'll be right behind him.

6 January, 1995

Someone got to Maguire before us!

I found Sinbad on the Parade, still determined to

give Kenny Maguire what for. He'd tucked this enormous spanner into his jacket for protection. To get him into real trouble, more likely.

There was no way I was going to let him go through with it on his own. Sinbad had a cab waiting. I decided to follow him. I had to go on the bus, but Maguire's office is only about a quarter of an hour's ride away.

The place was deserted, when I got there. No sign of life – Sinbad's or Maguire's! Maguire's little hideaway was on the first floor. I was scared to death climbing up the stairs. I half-expected to hear them arguing – I couldn't have been more than ten minutes behind Sinbad – but it was totally silent.

The door was open and I could see there'd been some sort of fight. Letters, files, bills, all sorts of things had been thrown on the floor.

I kind of crept into the room with my back to the wall. As soon as I was properly inside, this figure leapt at me, waving a big metal thing in my face.

Sinbad and his spanner! Practically frightened me to death!!

When I looked past him, I saw Kenny Maguire laid out on the floor. It was as if someone had pushed him hard up against the wall and literally punched his lights out. At first, I thought he was dead, until I noticed blood trickling down his face. He'll live.

Sinbad swore he hadn't laid a finger on him. His bottle had gone before he'd even got there, but he'd made his mind up to force Maguire to take the money anyway, somehow or other. In the end, all the agonizing was pointless. Maguire and the room had already been done over.

I didn't want to leave him lying there, unconscious, but Sinbad dragged me away. First he peeled off a tenner and put it in Maguire's jacket pocket. That's the last money he's ever going to get out of Sinbad OR Mum.

Sinbad's hard mood didn't last long. He let me telephone for an ambulance from the cab rank. I didn't give my name or anything, just that somebody had got hurt. We waited till we heard the sirens before we got into a taxi.

I don't know what we'd do without Sinbad. He's the best friend this family's ever had. The world has a new hero – CHAMOIS MAN!!!

We've agreed not to say a word to Mum!

7 January, 1995

Viv's number's been burning a hole in my pocket. Actually, I don't need the piece of paper any more. I know it off by heart already.

Should I?

Shouldn't I?

FOR
1. She's friendly and relaxed and looks like she'd be a lot of fun.

2. She's my own age.
3. She's made it pretty clear she'd like to get to know me.
4. I really fancy her.

AGAINST
1. I said I was giving up on relationships. Forever.
2. I might have read the signals wrong and she might knock me back.

Number 1 could easily be about having relationships with lecturers and number 2 is just me being paranoid. If she didn't want me to contact her, she wouldn't have given me her phone number.

The ayes have it. I'll call her before I go to work this evening.

8 January, 1995

Viv could be the one.

No. I'm *not* going to let myself get completely stupid about her.

If I can.

I haven't had such a good time in ages. I got paid today, so I popped into Grants and Viv picked me up from there. She's got this battered old Metro. Not so stylish as a trendy 2CV perhaps, but it goes. More or less.

There's a gay pub near Viv's place where we had a

couple of drinks. We gassed for the entire evening. Funny thing is, I can't remember a single thing we discussed. It wasn't like being with Chris, where everything had to be deep and meaningful. Viv just likes messing about. It was brilliant! I actually felt like I was 19 for once, instead of 39.

Viv dropped me back at the Parade. I was a bit worried about her driving me all the way home, in case Mum came out and wanted to meet her. God, the embarrassment! I still shudder when I remember Chris and the baby photos!!

We had a quick kiss – I really wanted to snog her, but it felt dead awkward. Quite apart from the fact some nosy member of the Brookside Residents Association might have been wandering around, I'm still getting used to being what I am. Besides, we'd only just met.

Viv was fine about it. She just smiled and asked to see me again. We're going out again tomorrow.

And the next day and the next and the next if I have my way.

10 January, 1995

I didn't realize! Am I stupid or what?

It was first day back at uni today. I was really looking forward to it. Seeing all me mates – and Viv. Mike was on the Parade, but he was in a funny mood. Like he was giving me the cold shoulder.

Turned out he'd seen me and Viv snogging on the Parade. He acted like he was all offended. Complained about us being 'a bit public'. Just as well he was the only one watching! I assumed it was a bit of a joke, only Mike started getting serious.

How could I not have noticed? All this time I thought we were good friends. Mates. We talked about everything. Shared secrets. I cried on his shoulder. He cried on mine. That's what friends do, isn't it?

Turns out Mike thought we were going out together. Even knowing what I am. A Lesbian. At first, I was furious with him. Typical bloody man. Thinking he could straighten me out. Give me a good old-fashioned seeing to. Show me what I've been missing. As if I didn't know.

Why is it people assume being gay is something I can switch off at a moment's notice?

It would be so much easier if Mike did just want to get into my knickers. But it's more than that. He said he's mad about me and he thought I felt the same way. How could I? I had no idea he even fancied me. Love didn't come into it. Not for me, at any rate.

He looked so hurt. Like he wanted to burst into tears. Only being a macho man standing in the middle of a shopping parade, he couldn't. There was nothing I could do or say. I feel as if it's all my fault, but I don't know what I should have done differently. I missed all the signs.

It's so sad. We were such good friends and now it's all spoilt.

11 January, 1995

Sinbad decided to tell Mum about Kenny Maguire's terrible fate. She was getting so worked up about it, he had no choice. He wanted me to be there for moral support. I didn't realize how much he'd need it.

I honestly thought Mum would be pleased. No more debt. No more debt collectors. Only she wasn't. When Sinbad told her how we'd found him, she was horrified. No way would she take the money. Blood money, she called it.

It didn't matter that what happened to that toerag had nothing to do with us. All those years with Dad have made her terrified of even the hint of violence. I should have realized. That time she hit Rachel, she was completely disgusted with herself. Now, she's disgusted with us.

According to her, nobody deserves to get beaten up. Nobody. Not even someone who bullies and bleeds people dry. That was the straw that broke the window cleaner's back. Sinbad flung the money on the couch and was about to walk out.

Something snapped inside me. I couldn't stand one more moment of the two of them winding each other up. I just wanted them to stop shouting and start talking.

The door of the extension was open. I shoved them through and turned the key. I actually locked my own mother and Sinbad in a room together.

It was such a relief. If they were stuck in there for a

while, I figured they'd have to discuss things properly. Get everything sorted out. They hammered on the door, but no way was I going to open it for at least two hours.

Instead I went round to Viv's. Not that I told her what I was up to. When I got back, the house was totally silent and dark. There was no light coming from under the extension door. A good sign, I thought. I opened the door really slowly, in case I was interrupting something.

It didn't work! They were on opposite sides of the room. Mum was sitting on the bed and Sinbad was leaning against the wall. He wouldn't look at her – or me. He just walked out of the back door and out of our lives.

Mum was devastated. All she could say was that she'd lost him. The only man who's ever really cared for her and he's gone. This business with Maguire has finished them. She's driven Sinbad away.

12 January, 1995

Happy Christmas to us!
Honestly!
Just goes to show – you can't keep a good man down. Sinbad wasn't driven away. He was just making a strategic withdrawal to regroup. Since he wasn't here for boring, ordinary Christmas in December, he

decided we'd have a special mega-Christmas in the middle of January.

Why not?

He brought all the trimmings round – turkey, stuffing, vegetables, decorations, crackers and, of course, a Christmas tree with lights. He even put a set of lights on the fir tree outside the front door.

When Mum came in, Rachel and I beat a hasty retreat upstairs. We came down half an hour later and there they were, cuddling in the kitchen, wearing party hats. No need for mistletoe there!

It's great to have him back. We're a proper family now. Why couldn't Sinbad have been my real Dad? When he's around, Mum starts to come out of her shell, get a bit of confidence back.

Christmas dinner was wonderful. I'm so stuffed I can hardly pick up my pen. Sinbad bought us all something. I got a sweatshirt and Rachel got footie boots. How did Sinbad know what she wanted, she asked. Easy. She's been nagging Mum about them non-stop for a year!

Mum got a watch. Small and gold and precious. A permanent present to remember the giver by. I hope. The two of them gazed into each other's eyes a lot. They hardly heard a word Rach and I were saying.

Best of all, Sinbad's got tickets for a holiday to Ireland. Rachel's being allowed to skive off school for a few days. Unfortunately, I can't afford to miss all those lectures. They're going to have to count me out.

What a shame! Not that I wouldn't fancy a holiday

on the Emerald Isle – but with them away, I can have the house to myself. Who knows? If I get lonely, I might just invite a friend to stay.

Can't think of a better way to spend a few days, myself.

13 January, 1995

Mike's avoiding me. Every time we pass on the Parade, he ducks into the nearest shop. It's so stupid! He can't go on avoiding me forever. I can't help what I am. I don't want to. Why can't we be friends? It's like something out of *When Harry Met Sally*.

I finally cornered him in the tunnel by the Pizza Parlour. I told him how sorry I was if I led him on. Maybe I shouldn't have let myself get so close to him. He was so sweet – said how much he liked me, that I look good, etc., etc. I would have been pleased if I hadn't been so uncomfortable. Knocking back someone like that Carl Banks would have been a cinch, but Mike's completely genuine. A great guy. I really don't want us to fall out.

Mike said he thought I might change my mind. If it was as easy as that, he's exactly the kind of fella I'd go for. I told him that although I'm not sure it was a good idea. Still, at least he smiled and shook my hand.

We're mates again, but next time, I'll be *very* careful about getting too close.

14 January, 1995

While the cats are away, this mouse is going to play! Viv and I went out to this little country pub for a quiet drink. She's such a laugh. Really easy-going and fun and relaxed. In fact, just what I need after Chris. Not that she's brain-dead or anything. Only sometimes it's nice not to talk sexual politics ALL the time.

Guess who was in the pub? Only Mike Dixon – with a woman! Nice bit of gossip here. The woman was Carl Banks' ex-wife, Sarah. Poor Mike looked like he'd been found out. I suppose it could look a bit bad – him going off with his mate's ex. The pub's so off the beaten track, he must have thought he was away from prying eyes. He said he thought 'you' (i.e. lesbians) had 'special' pubs (i.e. dark, hidden places where we can indulge our nasty appetites in private.) Sometimes, he can be a bit of a prat.

Still, his secret is safe with me!

Viv said she'd come over to dinner next week. And breakfast, too, I hope. She quite fancies Mike, which gave me a bit of a shock. Apparently, she swings both ways. She swore it doesn't mean she jumps into bed with anyone and that she's into seeing just one person at a time.

19 January, 1995

Viv finally came round to dinner. That girl has FAR

too good a social life! Which is fine when it includes me, but it doesn't always. Everyone likes her – straight men, gay men, straight women and, of course, gay women. There's something about her face that makes everyone relax. Perhaps it's the big blue eyes and wide red mouth. Every time she smiles I want to kiss her. Her hair's wonderful too – long and blonde. Normally it's tied back in these demure little plaits. What I want to know is, who's she trying to kid? At first, she looks incredibly innocent and naïve. When you get close up, there's this naughty little twinkle in her eye.

But as soon as we sat down the phone rang! Mum wanting to know if her little girl was managing. Viv was terrible. Kept kissing me and nibbling my ear while I was trying to hold a normal conversation. Then somebody rang the doorbell and we ended up cowering under the window so as not to be seen. Mum wouldn't be exactly thrilled if she found out I had a girlfriend staying.

The next thing is a noise out the back. This place is unbelievable! Neighbourhood watch is one thing. Sheer nosiness is quite another. First, that Jimmy Corkhill turned up with his mangy dog. It's some sort of cross between a pit-bull and a hog! The revolting animal (Cracker, not Corkhill) started sniffing around the patio stones. I was petrified. Especially when the other revolting animal (Corkhill, not Cracker) said there must be something buried under there. Then David Crosbie and Max Farnham turn up, complete with official torch. The Brookside Resident's Association doing its job – minding other people's business.

I got rid of them, but I'm so sick of it. Sick of living here. Sick of people sticking their nose in and wanting to know where I am and what I'm doing and who I'm with all the time. It's like living in a goldfish bowl.

20 January, 1995

Everything's so simple to Viv. Her answer – move out. Why not? She doesn't understand – and I can hardly explain! She must think I'm such a big baby, still living with my mother. There's a couple of rooms free at her place and she suggested I move in with her.

I can't think of anything I want more. But how can I leave home? I've had to be so practical with Mum on her own. Will I be able to afford it? What if we split up?

In the end, I agreed to stay with Viv for the weekend. I'd get to see the rooms and meet the others. I know without seeing it that I'd love to move in with her. To be a normal student and just start enjoying life.

What really decided me to go away for the weekend was Eddie Banks. His garden's three feet under water and he's decided it's something to do with us! Could he take a look under our flags? Oh yes. Of course. Come in. Dig them up. Oh look, what's this? The murdered body of Beth's father. . . .

I told him to get lost, but the whole thing really upset me. I was really looking forward to Viv and me having the weekend to ourselves without anyone interfering. It's impossible round here.

I'm going round to Viv's. It's hopeless trying to get a bit of peace round here.

23 January, 1995

I feel like I've been let out of prison! This weekend was really brilliant. I can't remember the last time I had a laugh. Even with Chris. Everything was always serious with her. Politics and that are important, but maybe the age thing was more of an issue than I thought. Basically, I just want to let my hair down a bit.

For the first time in my life, I feel normal. A normal student doing normal studenty thing. Who knows? I may even dress up as a clown and do something stupid for rag day.

I'm going to move out. Mum'll be fine. Viv's right – she's got Sinbad and Rachel. She doesn't need me around so much and I need my own space. Mum and Sinbad are getting on brilliantly. They'll probably be glad to have me out of the way.

I can't really afford it. But then, no-one can. It's student loan city round at Viv's. Everyone's doing bar or shop work. With what I get at Grant's, I can manage. Just.

As soon as Mum gets back from Ireland, I'm going to tell her.

24 January, 1995

Viv and I went into town this afternoon. When we got home, Eddie and Carl Banks were in our garden, digging up the patio.

I went mad. How dare they trespass!! Who do they think they are? This is private property. Everyone round here thinks they can just barge in whenever they like.

They'd dug right where the body's buried. There was a huge hole inches away from it. Viv and I ended up out there in the dark putting the flags back.

Now I can't move out. There's no way I can leave Mum on her own. I don't know what I was thinking about in the first place. How can I go? He's got us right where he wants us. I'll never get away from him. Even dead he's controlling our lives.

All I wanted was to be on my own. I told Viv to go. It must have sounded so weird, but I could hardly explain. She looked so hurt. She put the spade down, shrugged and left.

As soon as she was gone, I collapsed. Slid down into the mud and cried and cried and cried. My hands and face and clothes were covered in revolting slime, like I was trying to bury myself.

What if I hadn't been here? What if I hadn't come back and stopped them? Eddie's going to call someone round to look at it. They could come round tomorrow. And even if they don't, it's only a matter of time before they find him.

I wanted to howl at the top of my voice, but I couldn't. Supposing the neighbours heard?

25 January, 1995

Viv came round first thing this morning. She'd thought I wanted to finish with her. As if! It's only her that's keeping me sane at the moment. We made it up, of course. I wish I could confide in her, though.

Mum and Sinbad got back OK. I was never more glad to see them. Sinbad went next door to sort something out with Eddie. Mum worried. I told her about me and Viv. She said it doesn't bother her, but she never was any good at lying.

Things still aren't right between her and Sinbad. They had a great time and got on and everything, but more as friends than as lovers. It's so sad! They deserve each other. They were made for each other. How many other men would stand by her after all that's happened? It must be love. But why does everything else have to get in the way?

26 January, 1995

It's getting worse. Sinbad couldn't persuade Eddie to change his mind, so a team of workmen are coming round tomorrow with a mechanical digger. They're going to dig up the whole garden until they find the problem.

There was only one thing for it. Get rid of Rachel for the night and move the body. The first part was easy enough. Rachel wanted to go to the pictures with some mates. She was amazed when Mum said 'yes' without any arguing.

It was awful, planning what to do. What if the neighbours heard? Where were we going to put him? How were we going to move him without a car? What sort of state would he be in?

In the end, we decided to get him into the extension until Rachel went to bed, then dump him in the woods. It was incredibly risky, but leaving him was worse.

We might as well have saved our breath. I might have known Mum couldn't go through with it. She sort of hovered while me and Sinbad got going with the spades. Every time the blade went into the ground, I thought I was going to throw up. And all the time, we had to keep up this constant stream of reassurance to stop Mum going hysterical.

It was no use. Mum panicked. Lost her head and started crying. She was so scared of what we were going to find. As though we'd dig up the body and he'd still be alive. Furious because we'd buried him. Strong and powerful and vicious. Ready to beat us all to a pulp.

Mum couldn't handle it. I couldn't bear to see her so upset, so we stopped. Put the flags back and crept into the house.

There's only one other option. We're going to have to get as far away from here as possible. Leave him and everything else behind. We're going to have to go on the run. It's our only chance.

27 January, 1995

It's unreal. Two days ago, I was thinking about moving in with Viv. Now, I'm on the Stena Hibernia, surrounded by luggage. Any minute now we'll be docking in Dun Laoghaire.

We watched the workmen from Mum's bedroom window. Sinbad, Mum and me. They had this huge excavator. We were concentrating so hard, it was like being hypnotized. My eyes wouldn't move. Each time the scoop thing went down, I held my breath and prayed they'd uncover a burst pipe or something. Waited for the shout that meant the problem had been found.

Nothing.

Next door's garden was a wreck. All Rosie's flower beds and the lawn had gone, leaving a great sludge of mud and stagnant water. Gradually the machine moved closer and closer to our fence.

I could feel a hot lump of panic blocking my throat and chest. I forced my eyes to turn away and my mouth to open. We had to pack. No point in waiting around.

Sinbad decided we should go to Ireland. Hardly Australia, but it's big enough to lie low in for a while. And we can get English papers easily enough. Find out what's happening.

He was great, really organized and calm, even though I could see he was as worried as I was. Mum and I were detailed to collect Rachel, while he took the rest of his money out of the building society.

Mum and I threw everything into suitcases. Clothes, washing stuff, books, whatever might come in handy, until there wasn't room to cram another thing in. All the while Mum went on and on and on.

'I've ruined everything. This is the end. What about university? What about Rachel's GCSE's? How did we think we could ever get away with it?

What have I done?

What have I done?

What have I done?

I had to keep sane and positive, even though I wanted to scream. For all we know, they might not even find the body. We might be able to come back in a few days. If we can just hold on to that, maybe we'll survive.

Rachel was in Chemistry when we got back to the school. We told her Kenny Maguire was after us. I never thought I'd be glad that plonker existed! Poor Rach. She was completely bewildered. Couldn't understand why we don't go to the police.

It's Sinbad's birthday today. We all forgot, except Rachel. She'd arranged a surprise party. At six o'clock this evening, all the neighbours are going to knock on our door, expecting sausage rolls and beer. Instead, we'll be in Ireland. Fugitives. On the run. With no idea of whether we'll ever be able to go back.

28 January, 1995

This is unreal. We've booked into a B&B in Dun Laoghaire. A happy family on a happy family holiday. Bit too cold for sand-castles, but never mind. There's always walks on the prom.

Sinbad and I try to keep calm. We've got to. If we don't, we'll give ourselves away. Mum looks terrified the whole time and Rachel doesn't stop whingeing for a second. Between the two of them, I'm slowly going mad.

Mum had a nightmare about Dad. It was as much as Sinbad could do to stop her screaming the place down. She's going to pieces. Trouble is, this is Dad's country. Every time Mum hears the accent, she jumps. Like she's going to turn round and he'll be standing there. She's terrified we'll get caught. So terrified she's almost ready to give herself up.

We couldn't stay indoors. Rachel was cracking up and even Sinbad was getting nervy. We went for a walk along the prom. Bleak seashore just about sums it up. Rachel was getting more and more narky. From her point of view, it's completely stupid us being here. She just won't stop going on. 'When are we going back home? What about Lee? Have I got to go to a new school?' Sinbad and I were trying to calm her down, when we noticed Mum had vanished.

There was this bloke on the other side of the street. Mum only went up to him and called him Trevor. She's going to blow everything if she carries on accusing strangers of being her dead husband. Either Sinbad or I will have to stay with her the whole time. We can't afford to let her out of our sight. Or Rachel. She slipped off twice in the afternoon to try and phone Lee. She'll ruin everything.

Sinbad got hold of the papers. Nothing. If we can just hold on for a few days, give ourselves a bit of breathing space, it could all blow over. I'm *not* going to prison. Nor is Mum or Sinbad. Mum said it was ridiculous, us running away. But we couldn't sit there and watch them dig him up. We had to do something.

It's as if Mum's giving in. As if we did something wrong and we should have reported it. But what good would that have done? So they'd've locked him up for a while. A short while. Given us another safe house. He would have found us and the same thing would have happened again and again and again. It would never have stopped. He ruined our lives. All the beatings. What he did to me and Rachel.

If we give up now, hand ourselves meekly over to the police, he'll have won. I'm *never* going to let that happen. It was him or us. I don't regret anything we did. All I regret is that he was ever part of our lives.

29 January, 1995

Mum gave Sinbad the slip first thing this morning. She didn't go very far. Just down to the beach for a breath of fresh air, but Sinbad and I panicked. I had visions of her wandering into the police station.

Sinbad told me Mum even talked about killing herself. It makes me so angry. Dad's dominating our lives again. She'd even started to walk straighter before this blew up. Now, her tiny amount of self-confidence has vanished. She's gone right back to being frightened and shaking and incapable of doing a thing for herself.

Why can't she put a brave face on it? For Rachel's sake, at least. If we don't want Rachel or anyone else to know why we're here, she's going to have to act differently. Guilt's written all over her.

It's so hard, though. I'm terrified, too. I daren't let myself think about what would happen if they found the body. Every time I do, I want to be sick. Every moment I want to cry. Just sit down in the street and howl.

There's no-one to think about my feelings. I've given up as much as Mum and Rachel. I didn't get a chance to say goodbye to Viv. I try not to think about her, but I can't help it. She deserves an explanation after I walked out on her. What if she decides to go to the police and report me missing or something? Maybe I could write her a note or give her a quick call. I wouldn't tell her where we are, just that I'm OK. Maybe I could even trust her with the truth.

There was nothing in the papers again. Sinbad wants to go home if the body still hasn't been found. It's a bit too soon. We need a couple more days, just to be sure.

30 January, 1995

Rachel knows something's up. She's going to keep on until we tell her the truth. Perhaps we ought to tell her. Supposing they do find the body and she sees it in the papers or on the TV before we do?

We spent the day wandering round the beach again. It's unbelievable that you can be so bored and so scared all at the same time. There's nothing to do here. Even if there was, we couldn't concentrate on doing it.

While Sinbad and Rachel went off to get the papers, Mum and I had a heart-to-heart. I told her I was think-ing of contacting Viv. You'd've thought I'd suggested starting World War Three!

It all came out. What she really felt about me. I thought Mum was coming round a bit. That she was trying to understand. But she doesn't even begin to get it.

All the cliches came out –

> 'You're not really a Lesbian – *it's a phase.*
>
> *You're not really a Lesbian – it's a reaction to what your father did.*
>
> *You're not really a Lesbian – it's not natural*'.

She made me feel about three inches high. Like I was some tiny, little alien that had strayed on to a bizarre planet where nobody spoke my language. Couldn't even comprehend my gestures.

It's not a phase or a reaction. I can't explain what makes me feel this way. I just do. Maybe it's always been there. Deep down. I don't want to go out with boys and pretend, just to make Mum feel good. I'm content with myself. I've stopped fighting against it.

I'm a Lesbian. Glad to be gay and all that.

I want my mother to love me whatever I am. But she can't. Won't. There's all these strings and conditions.

How can she call me unnatural? My feelings are the most natural I've ever known. Only, according to Mum, it's not about emotions. It's about what we do. Physically.

She almost asked *that* question. What *do* Lesbians do in bed?

Nothing that I'm ashamed of.

All Mum wanted was a 'normal' family, she said. What did she get? A husband who sleeps with his daughters and a daughter who sleeps with other women.

That hurt most of all. Mum truly believes that I'm as twisted and evil as Dad.

What do *I* get? A Mum who sleeps with a man for money.

31 January, 1995

It's out. They've found him.

LIVERPOOL BIN BAG BODY MYSTERY

A decomposing corpse has been found buried under a suburban patio. The gruesome discovery was brought to light when water started pouring into shop steward, Eddie Banks' back garden. When he couldn't find the cause, Mr. Banks hired an excavator to dig up his garden and the one next door.

He was curious when a large bundle wrapped in black bin bags was revealed. Curiosity turned to horror when a corner of one bag split and the remains of a hand fell into his lap.

Mr. Banks' neighbours have vanished. Police are looking for housewife, Mrs. Amanda Jordache and her two teenage daughters, Elizabeth and Rachel. The body has not yet been identified'.

So that's it. We're on the run. Officially. Mum went to pieces of course. Sank down on the bed and wailed. For once in her life, I wish she'd just face things. If we can get our act together, maybe we can work something out.

Obviously, we can't go back home! But we've got a chance if we keep one step ahead of the police.

The first thing to do was to tell Rachel.

Mum tried to tell her, but in the end it was down to me. She couldn't handle it. Rachel went mad. Shouting and screaming. Hitting Mum. Not listening to a word beyond the fact that Mum killed him.

The strange thing is that she said Dad never touched her. But I saw him. Saw him in her bed with my own eyes. Her all innocent and trusting. Like I used to be. Thinking he loved her. Like I did.

She knows what he was like. Hitting Mum whenever he felt like it. He was a bully. He went to prison for it. And when he came out, he hadn't learned a thing, hadn't changed one bit. He just got worse and worse, until he threatened to kill us all. That's why we had to do it. It was the only way to stop him from what he did to us all.

Rachel ran off. Vanished into thin air.

Sinbad went one way. I went another. Mum stayed put to wait.

Half an hour later, there was still no sign of her, so we started to search. We must have gone up and down every street in Dun Laoghaire. I don't have the words to describe it. A nightmare. Each street looking exactly the same as the last. And the tiniest bit different. Strange streets. Odd Irish names, but familiar after three days of traipsing through. Friendly people smiling at us, frightening us to death because if they knew . . .

Mum wouldn't let us stop for a moment. Not even for a cup of tea. All the time, her voice nagged in my ear. Anything could have happened to her. Perhaps she went to the police. Perhaps she's thrown herself off a roof. Perhaps some pervert's picked her up off the street. Me denying each fear as soon as she said it. And the feeling in my stomach as I believed each fear as soon as I denied it.

We passed the Guarda station. Guarda. Hardly sounds like the police. Every time we pass an officer in the street, he smiles at us. Mum wanted to go in. Give herself up to find out what happened to my stupid little sister. I promised we'd find her. No way was she going to blow it.

Twice we went to the ferry station. The most logical thing was that she'd try to get home. The third time I spotted her. In a police car! We got back to the station ten minutes later.

The buy behind the desk was a real Dixon of Dock Green. All fatherly and jovial. Practically patted Rachel on the head. They were happy to write her little escapade off as a schoolgirl prank.

She came out in a sulk. Wouldn't look at any of us. I was terrified she'd give us away. The evening edition was on the front desk. Headline:

> 'WINDOW CLEANER WANTED IN BIN BAG BODY MYSTERY'.

Dun Laoghaire was dangerous. The town's far too small.

While the sergeant was finding the paperwork, we grabbed Rachel and ran. There was a bus to Dublin outside. Sinbad and I dragged Rachel and Mum on to it. No time to pick up our clothes or anything. We piled on as it was pulling away.

I'm sitting in yet another anonymous bed-and-breakfast place. I can't sleep. I can feel the nightmares lining up behind my eyes, ready to pounce on me if my eyelids so much as droop. Rachel hasn't said a word. Which is a relief. I'm so angry and frightened and lost, I couldn't cope with arguing with her.

How long can I keep it up? Pushing Mum on, pulling Rachel. If it wasn't for Sinbad, I'd've gone under days ago. Perhaps we should give ourselves up. But I'm not going to prison. Neither is Mum. I'm not going to let Dad win. He was so clever. Everyone thought the world of him. So cheery and gentle and kind. They didn't know what he was really like. They'll never believe it now.

We've got to keep going. As long as we're free, we're still in with a chance.

1 February, 1995

We're worth a whole page in the papers now. With pictures. Dad's been identified – *BUILDING SOCIETY MANAGER, TREVOR JORDACHE. VERY RESPECTABLE.* There was a picture of him. And a photo of our back garden, taken from next door, no doubt. So much for the honourable Eddie Banks.

They're digging up the body Mum identified. Even that poor old tramp in Dad's grave isn't allowed to rest in peace. The papers are trying to make out we had something to do with his death as well.

The police have sussed we're in Ireland. We're going to be on the wrong end of the biggest murder hunt since the Yorkshire Ripper came to town.

When Rachel saw Dad's picture, she went mad.

Started shouting for him at the breakfast table. Going out's risky, but staying in is worse.

More streets.

More parks.

Rachel finally started to talk about it. She wanted all the gory details – how we planned it, how we talked about it. And over and over. Again and again. Why? Why? Why?

She won't believe us. Even though she saw Dad beating the living daylights out of us so many times. Even though he got into bed with her. She still says he never laid a finger on her.

It's like what really happened won't go into her head, so she's rewriting the story. Her version is that Mum and Sinbad worked it out between them, so they could be together. He's become the villain. Rachel ended up screaming at him.

'It's you, all this, isn't it? Ordering us around. Getting into our house. Ruining it all. You made Mum do this, didn't you? You told her to kill him'.

She ran straight into a guarda. Started to tell him we're the people in the papers. Sinbad covered up. Said it was a bit of a domestic. Sisters fighting like cat and dog.

The chatted. Like everything was normal.

This could be a dream. Things like this don't happen. Not to ordinary people like me and Mum and Rachel and Sinbad. We're not gangsters. What do we know about being on the run? A medical student, a housewife, a schoolgirl and a window cleaner. How can we hope to get away with it?

2 February, 1995

They almost caught us last night. We booked into the Durgevale Hotel. Twice as expensive as the B&Bs in Dun Laoghaire, but more anonymous. I didn't think the receptionist had taken any notice of us. One of the advantages of being in a city – people ignore you. Only she was sharper than she looked.

Sinbad went down to get the papers hot off the press. Two seconds later he burst into our room, shouting that the bizzies were there. We got out of the fire escape and into an alley behind the hotel. They were after us. Really after us. Blowing whistles and ordering us to stop.

We ran in a straight line. Going nowhere as quickly as we could. A bloke was unloading crates of booze from a hatchback. Sinbad leapt in and turned the key. I shoved Mum into the front and got Rachel into the back with me. Sinbad was off before I'd even got the door closed. The boot was still open, so we left a trail of broken bottles behind us as we drove off. I could see the bloke in the rear view mirror, swearing at us and the guardais running back for their cars, radioing for help.

URGENT!!
URGENT!!
URGENT!!

Their cars were at the front of the hotel, so we lost

them easily. Sinbad dumped the car in a road somewhere. I've no idea where we are. We just booked into the first place we came to.

There's no point in even trying to sleep. Rachel's pretending, breathing in and out slowly so I'll think she's nodded off. This room is so lonely. We've none of our things here. Totally cut off from everything.

I wonder what Viv's doing now. She must have read in the papers about what happened. What must she think? We hardly had any time together. A few dates and one brilliant weekend. I wish I could call her to try and explain. Maybe she would understand.

Who are you kidding, Beth Jordache? By now, she's clubbing it with some new girl. Or bloke.

One thing less for me to worry about. Or one thing more.

I'm too tired to write. Too confused to think. I just want it to be all over.

But we've got out of Dublin as quickly as we can. Switching B&Bs isn't enough. For one thing, the money's running out. We've enough for a few more days, but only away from the capital. It's unbelievably expensive! Much worse than Liverpool.

Sinbad, Mum and I had a conference. Going back to England's out. We'd get caught as soon as we went near the ferry. Heading down the coast seemed a better idea. As long as we keep moving, we've got a chance to get ourselves out of this mess.

The only thing left is for us to go abroad. Cheap flights are easy to pick up. We can go from town to town and try to pick up work on the way. Dishwashing. Behind a bar. All of us can do that. We'll have to save up enough to get right away. The main problem is how to get passports.

Mum was being totally defeatist. But it's either that or plan B.

Plan B. Give up. Go to jail. Let Dad win.

No way.

3 February, 1995

Rachel's being impossible. I don't know how much longer I can cope. It's doing my head in. She's determined not to believe us. Her versions are getting more and more bizarre. The latest thing is she thinks we killed Dad for the insurance money.

What insurance money??? After all the money problems we've had, she should realize we haven't got a bean.

We can't drag her around like some kind of hostage. Every day, she tells Mum how much she hates her, but there must be something holding her back. Sooner or later, she'll land us all in it, though. She's getting farther and farther away from us.

I'm writing this in a restaurant in Wexford. To be precise, in a loo in a restaurant in Wexford. I had to escape for a few minutes. Sinbad and Mum are having this stupid discussion about who should take the blame.

Mum: I did it. I'll say it was me. You and Beth

keep out of it.

    Sinbad: Why don't I say it was me? We were in the
                house. He caught us together. I lost me rag
                and . . .

    Mum: If anyone confesses, it should be me.

    Sinbad: No, me.

    Mum: Me.

Round and round. I can't eat. I can't think straight. Two minutes and I'll have to go back.

No-one's going to confess anything. Not if I can help it.

4 February, 1995

I've been re-reading what I wrote. Talk about famous last words. They caught us half an hour after that. There was a guarda reading a paper at the bar of the restaurant. Mum kept looking over at him. Guilt was scrawled all over her face. Rachel went on and on at her to give herself up. Get it over with. Tell them what we've done.

Eventually, he left. We were about to go and find somewhere for the night when we heard all these sirens. Suddenly, the place was full of police. And this time, they weren't looking friendly!

Rachel yelled at the top of her voice.

'You killed my dad. You stabbed him. You killed my dad.'

After that, we didn't stand a chance. We tried. Sinbad and I grabbed Mum's hands and crashed her through the kitchens. Pans everywhere. Boiling water. Saucepans. Gravy and chip fat on the floor. Everyone shouting. I looked over my shoulder. All I could see were bewildered white uniforms. Kitchen staff not knowing what was going on. Then the blue uniforms came chasing after us.

More of them were waiting for us at the back door. Two policewomen pulled me away. I couldn't hear what they said. My ears were buzzing and there was all red in front of my eyes.

Squashed in the back of a police car. A guarda either side of me. Saying nothing. Mum and Sinbad in separate cars. Driven away.

I don't know where. They won't tell me. I don't know where they are. I've lost them.

MUM!!

This cell. It's just like I always imagined a cell to be. Bare and dark. Grey-painted brick. Only I never added the cold or the stench for myself. The toilet in the corner sinks. My fear smells worse. I put my hand against the wall, expecting it to be damp. But it was me sweating out terror.

5 February, 1995

I saw him last night. It was quiet. Silent as the grave. '*How's my little girl? My Beth*'.

Th' Irish lilt, same as we've been hearing all week. But not friendly. Threatening. My stomach churns when I see the look on his face. The false smile that means 'you're for it now'.

'You shouldn't have done it. You and your mother. Very naughty'.

He wags his finger. Shakes his head at me. Revolves so I can see the hole in his back, the blood spreading red over the cotton.

I try to scream. My mouth opens, but no sound comes out. He's standing over me. Raising his arm, making a fist in slow motion. I can hear my own blood rushing past my ears.

'I'm going to kill you. Kill you. Kill you'.

His fist comes crashing down. The world goes black and I know I'm going to die.

I heard screams. Loud, terrified shrieks. I was awake and the noise was coming from me. No-one came. They let me go on and on until my throat was stinging. I didn't dare lie down again. Instead, I stood against the wall, waiting for the light, watching as the shadows from the bars started to appear and reach longer and longer across the floor.

They won't let me see Mum or Sinbad or Rachel. Suppose Mum heard me. Suppose she spent the night screaming the place down as well, only too far away for me to hear. Suppose she can't stand it. Suppose she does something – drastic. Suppose I never see her again.

6 February, 1995

They moved us back to Liverpool this afternoon. A procession of police cars drove out of the station and on to the ferry. The one I was in led the way. I didn't dare turn round to see if Mum and the others were following.

When we got on board, I caught a glimpse of Mum. She looked as if she hadn't slept or eaten or washed for a month. Then this hatchet-faced cow pushed me into a cabin and locked the door. We sat there while the boat lurched about, not saying a word.

It's hard to believe we were only caught the night before last. I don't know which is worse – the fear or the boredom. Back in England, we were driven to a police station in Liverpool and locked up again. They're going to start interviewing us in the morning.

I can have a solicitor there if I want, but I don't. When I saw Mum, looking so awful, I made up my mind. There's no way she's going to prison. She may have pushed the knife in, but it was because of me. If Dad hadn't been beating me to a pulp, she'd never have done it. It was my idea to kill him in the first place, mine to try and poison him. My fault because I goaded him into attacking me. That's why she attacked him.

Mum couldn't stand prison, being away from Sinbad and Rachel. She wouldn't survive. She'd go mad. People do. They go inside perfectly sane and it warps them. Except bastards like Dad. It couldn't affect him – he was twisted already.

If anyone's going to prison, it'll be me. I'm the strong one. I can stand it. Even if I get life, there'll be parole. I'll still have years left to live when I get out.

I've worked my story out. I'll tell the truth as far as I can – that he was drunk and beating me. When his back was turned, I grabbed a knife and stabbed him in the back. It's completely possible. I buried him that night, after everyone had gone to bed. Mum didn't know a thing.

7 February, 1995

They made me wait for hours. I don't know about Sinbad, but they definitely interviewed Mum before me, because they knew about Dad raping me.

How can a simple little room be so terrifying? There was a table with two chairs. Detective Inspector Coban sat on one side, I was on the other. A policewoman stood to attention behind me. She was supposed to be there to make sure everything was above board. I could almost feel her breathing, though she was the other end of the room. Standing behind me. Judging me. Hating me.

The whole thing was formal and quiet and terrifying. I felt like I was being hypnotized by the cassette tape going round and round. I told him about Dad. How he used to terrorize us. How he said he would kill us.

And what I did about it.

Detective Inspector Coban sat there and asked all these stupid questions.

Why didn't I report Dad to the police when he raped me?

Because I was only fourteen. I told my mum. I was a kid. What else did he expect?

Did Dad interfere with me after he came out of prison?

No. Because by then I wasn't a kid any more. I kept out of his way and he went after Rachel instead.

Why did I kill him?

To stop him doing to Rachel what he did to me. And to stop him from killing him.

He didn't believe me. Even about Dad raping me. His eyes didn't change and his voice was steady the whole time. Like it was some ritual he had to perform, even though he really knew everything.

Then they took me back to my cell. Home from home – I don't think! He's just been in again. Mum's confessed to being the murderer. So has Sinbad. They're going to carry on questioning us tomorrow.

8 February, 1995

If I can just hold out a bit longer, they'll have to let us go. I'm sure there are rules about how long they can keep someone on remand before they charge them. We've already been here days as it is.

I was back in the interview room again this morning.

The questions were worse. Even though I'd been trying to work out what they'd ask, I still got confused.

How did I drag a fully-grown man outside and bury him three feet deep without anyone seeing and without anyone helping?

How did I convince Mum that a total stranger was her husband?

I made up some stuff about Mum being really disturbed at the time, so she hardly looked at the body or the things.

He's worked it out, though. Realized that me and Mum killed Dad together and took advantage of the other body being found. The only thing he doesn't know is who pushed the knife in.

They know about the poison, too. He asked me if I knew anything about toxicology. The effect of poisonous substances on the human body. I told him I gave Dad the weed-killer, but he wouldn't listen.

Eventually, I broke down in tears. There was nothing else I could do. He let me go back to the cells, but we're going out this afternoon. I don't know where.

Later

After lunch, DI Coban and his friends took me and Mum out of the police station. We went in separate cars again. It felt weird being outside again, after a week behind locked doors. Hoards of reporters swooped down on us. Vultures prodding us with microphones and sharp pencils.

The police put green blankets over our heads, the kind that are made out of a sort of mesh. They smelt revolting, all sweat and urine, but it was better than being mauled about by the gutter press.

He took us to the rubbish dump. The cars were parked on this hill overlooking it. When Mum got out of her car, I thought she was going to collapse. We stood there looking at it. Acres of rubbish. Rubbish from houses, schools, restaurants. Everywhere. All the bin bags of Liverpool end up there. And the noise. Lorries turning and unloading. Thousands of seagulls screeching and scavenging in the muck.

The council keeps a register. A chunky red folder with a record of every load of rubbish that's ever been dumped. The date, the tonnage, which street it came from and where they buried it.

Mum told me about putting the knife out for the bin men. Sooner or later the police are going to find it. It could be weeks. It could be months.

They made us walk through it. I thought I'd be sick from the smell. I had to keep my scarf tied round my nose and mouth. Every step we took, a cloud of flies and insects swarmed up. The piles of rubbish moved as though they were alive and decomposing in front of our eyes.

It was too much for Mum. She blurted it out. That we tried to poison him, only it didn't work. He beat me, so Mum put the knife in his back. Then they drove us back to the station.

9 February, 1995

We were charged this morning. Mum's down for murder and conspiracy to murder. I'm being done for conspiracy.

> *Elizabeth Jordache. You are charged that at Brookside Close, Manor Park in the county of Merseyside on or about the 7th May, 1993, you did conspire to murder Trevor Jordache, contrary to common law. If you wish to say anything, I must warn you that what you do say may be written down and used in evidence. Do you have anything to say in relation to the charge?*

I kept my mouth shut. What was there to say?

At least I've found out what's happened to the others. Rachel's staying with the Banks's. Sinbad's been let go. God knows where he is, though. They still won't let us see him.

There's a bail hearing tomorrow. The police have got a solicitor to represent us. I spoke to him and he was quite sympathetic. He's going to lay it on thick about close ties with the community, and me studying, and Rachel needing to be looked after. We haven't got a cat in hell's chance of being let out, though.

10 February, 1995

The first bit of luck we've had since this whole sordid business began!! We've been granted bail!!!

The court room was terrifying. Mum and I sat in the dock, flanked by policewomen and behind sheets of bullet-proof glass. Imprisoned or cocooned? I'm not sure if it was to keep us in or other people out. We were on show. Exhibits in the Chamber Of Horrors.

ROLL UP! ROLL UP! SEE THE WARPED MOTHER AND DAUGHTER WHO POISONED AND STABBED THE BEST HUSBAND AND FATHER THAT EVER LIVED!!!

Sinbad slipped into the court just as the hearing started. I was incredibly relieved to see him. Somewhere in the back of my mind there'd been the tiniest thought that he might have skipped. I should have known better. He sat there with his fingers crossed, holding his breath. Not moving a muscle.

The whole thing was very low-key. Nothing like LA Law or the O J Simpson trial with power-dressed lawyers cracking their cheekbones to

OBJECTION!
OVERRULED!!
OBJECTION!
OVERRULED!!

The prosecution went first. They didn't say anything about us having mucked them around and lying. I suppose that's for the trial itself. DI Coban stood up and gave us this look. Straight and hard. No emotion. For a minute, I couldn't make myself breathe. It was like we were jungle animals that the great hunter had captured and defeated. I could have coped with disgust – hatred, even – but that . . .

The solicitor was brilliant. The prosecution started going on about how we'd gone on the run. Then, our guy stood up and, in an ordinary voice, said that they couldn't ask DI Coban that, because he'd been in England and it was just hearsay.

Hearsay!!!

Heard in every bloody paper in the land! But that doesn't make it true in a court of law. So nothing – not a single thing – was said about the week we were in Ireland. The prosecution looked pig-sick. They hadn't bothered to fetch any guardais in. Serve them right for being incompetent.

Our defence went on about me being a medical student and Mum having a job and Rachel needing looking after. His voice was dead convincing – sincere and normal. It sounded much more real than the prosecution bloke declaiming like he was spouting Shakespeare.

The summing up droned on for ages. The magistrate really loved the sound of his own voice. Talk about a power trip. He repeated everything the prosecution had said.

I wanted him to get it over with. We hadn't got a chance, so why prolong the agony? Sling us back behind bars. Where we belong.

Then he went on to the defence.

'The primary concern of the prosecution is that if bail were granted, the defendants would abscond. Is there anything to allay this fear?'

He repeated all the reasons why we wouldn't run away. How we'd been of previous good character. Lived for years at the same address. Strong ties with the local community. If anyone is speaking to us after this! It sounded pretty feeble – even to me. Mum was sinking down on the bench beside me. I held her hand while the magistrate gave the verdict.

'It is the opinion of the court that the defendants would be most unlikely to jeopardize all this by failing to surrender to custody at the appropriate time. Accordingly, bail is granted under the conditions that the defendants shall surrender their passports, bail to be fixed at £10,000 each'.

That was it! Free to go. DI Coban looked gobsmacked. He stormed out of the court-room, looking like he wanted to hit the usher. Maybe the magistrate thought we couldn't raise the money, but Sinbad's signed over his house as surety.

We met up with Sinbad outside the court. We stood there in this big waiting-hall hugging each other as if we'd never let go. If only Sinbad had been my Dad . . .

Barry Grant has come up trumps. We're staying at his place until the police release number 10. He's even said I can have my job back at Grants. I can go in as soon as I'm ready. God knows when that'll be.

Sinbad made supper, but I couldn't face food. My stomach was churning. I hadn't realized how terrified I was that they'd lock us up in That Place.

How long before they lock us up again? The solicitor said it could be ages for the trial to come up. Till then there's nothing we can do except wait.

12 February, 1995

Life at Barry's is scary, depressing and very, very boring. I can't concentrate on anything. Can't talk to Mum and Sinbad. There's only one subject. Round and round. One minute, we're going to get off scot free. The next, they're going to bang us up and throw away the key.

The papers are still full of the story. Every morning, a load of reporters and photographers flock to our house. The only funny thing about the whole mess is that they haven't realized we're actually camped out across the road.

Mum's biggest headache is Rachel. She's worried sick about it. The little cow won't speak to her. The other night, Mum sneaked over to the Banks's house when the gutter press staggered off down the boozer. Rachel wouldn't let her in. Kept the chain on the door and hurled abuse through the letterbox.

'I HATE YOU. I HATE YOU AND I HATE BETH. I DIDN'T WANT THEM TO LET YOU OUT

OF PRISON, BECAUSE I NEVER WANTED TO
SEE YOU OR HER AGAIN.'

Mum was shattered. All she can think about is how
to see her. To try and explain. Make her understand.
She spends the whole day at the window, watching the
Banks's house. When it goes quiet, she's convinced
they've taken my stupid sister away.

I could kill Rachel. How dare she make Mum suffer
like this! Her own mother. Why this fixation with Dad?
How come he's always the good guy to her? After what
he did to her. Did to us all.

I don't want her to come back. I can't bear what
she's doing to Mum, but part of me's glad. The longer
she keeps sulking, the longer she stays away.

14 February, 1995

The police unsealed the house yesterday and we're
back home. A bit dingy and dusty, but basically the
same as when we left it. You can tell we left in a hurry.
There were a couple of pints of milk stinking the fridge
out.

It's only just over a fortnight since we left. I can't
believe how much has happened. Uni and Viv and
everything seem like a past life on another planet. How
are we ever going to get back to normal?

I completely forgot it was Valentine's day. Sinbad
didn't get Mum a card. I didn't get one for Viv. She

didn't send me one. I really want to phone her, but I'm terrified of what she'll say.

I can't ask her to keep seeing me. What's in it for her? Years and years of prison visiting. Everyone pointing the finger. Not having a life of her own. I'm trouble. My whole family is. There's no point in expecting her to stand by me. I can't drag her into all this. It's not as if it was the romance of the century.

It could have been, though.

15 February, 1995

'BODY IN GARDEN: GIRL IN GAY SEX STORM'

or how about

'GAY LOVE SECRET OF MURDER SUSPECT'

Every time I open a paper, I find out something new about myself. Now it's that I killed Dad because I'm gay. In fact, me and Mum are a pair of murdering dykes. Two man-hating women killed a poor, defenceless, good father. Trial by press. And we've been found guilty as hell.

I wonder which one of our salt-of-the-earth neighbours gave them this lovely snippet. No, sold it to them. They've got what they wanted at last. My private life splashed all over the front page. How can they print this stuff? It's disgusting. They don't care who they hurt as long as they sell papers.

Viv came round. Mum was dead shirty with her. Sort of nodded without saying anything. It was bad enough before. All this crap in the papers hasn't exactly improved her attitude.

We went out into the garden to talk. She wanted to be there for me. Part of me desperately wanted to reach out for her. It would be such a relief to have someone on my side, who doesn't need propping up all the time.

I couldn't do it. I couldn't even look her in the face. All the while we were talking, I kept my eyes fixed on the back fence. I can't handle a relationship as well as everything else at the moment. I feel guilty enough about what I've done to her as it is. Anyone who gets mixed up with me is bound to regret it.

Viv asked me if it was true. Not about being gay – she knows that!! But about Dad. I said it was and then she didn't know what to say. So I told her to go. We hugged and said goodbye and now she's not part of my life any more.

17 *February, 1995*

I can't stop thinking about Viv. Was I right to finish with her? Could she have coped? Could I?

Maybe she would have been on our side. God knows, we're going to need some support. The more I go over and over our last conversation, the more I'm convinced she might have understood. Now, I can remember a couple of things she said, but yesterday it's like I simply didn't hear them.

'They're not going to lock you up, are they? Not when they hear what you've done'.

The trouble is, they *can* just lock us up. It's happened to women before, even when there's been heaps of protests. There's this group – Women for Justice – who've been campaigning to get a woman released that killed her husband. He'd tortured and beaten and raped her for years and years and years. She was so terrified of him, she killed him. Only, because she used a weapon, the police said it was premeditated and she was banged up for life.

That could happen to us.

It's not fair!

How can we get a fair trial with the gutter press foaming at the mouth? Two man-hating women killed a poor, defenceless, good, father. One of them a lesbian. A hanging offence, according to the Sun. That's how they'll put it. Man's justice in a man's world.

'You can't just give up.'

That was the other thing Viv said to me. Well, we're not going to. I'm never going to let him win. This family is going to get back to normal. When we get to court, Mum and I will tell the world what he did. Why we *had* to kill him. Why we had no choice.

Until then, it's business as usual. I'm going back to uni. I've got loads of work to catch up on. So I can become a doctor, not a prisoner. No matter what. Our only chance is to be positive and face them all. We can cope with a few dirty looks and whispers.

18 February, 1995

Rachel still refuses to speak to us. It's ridiculous. We're next door and she blanks Mum every time she sets foot in the garden. Poor Mum's going through hell! Every time she thinks Rachel might possibly be within sight, she rushes out to try and talk to her. Every time she ends up in tears, because my stupid sister turns her back. I don't know what Rachel's up to. Can't she see what she's doing to her own mother?

I couldn't bear to see Mum destroying herself like that, so I went next door to have it out with Rachel. She tried to avoid me by running upstairs to the Banks's spare room, but a door slammed in my face was the least of my worries.

I asked her why she's doing this to Mum, why she's making her suffer?

Rachel said it was because Mum made Dad suffer. What about what he did to us? To me and Mum. And to her. I saw it. I saw him with my own eyes. Him in bed with her. But Rachel denies it every time. Accused *me* of lying, because I'm gay.

What's going on in her mind? It's like everything's got twisted up. Dad could do no wrong in her eyes. As far as she's concerned, he loved her and would never do anything to harm her. Therefore, we're the ones who are lying. And because I'm a Lesbian, I must hate men.

That's what she said: 'You hate men and that's why you hated my Dad'.

Always *my* dad. Never *our* dad.

She was the one that told the reporter about me being gay.

I didn't realize how much she hates me. How much she hates what I am. What else could I say? I just turned on my heel and left.

20 February, 1995

Prison can't be worse than this! I tried to do some revision, seeing as I'm DEFINITELY going in tomorrow, but I couldn't concentrate. Mum won't leave the house. I can't bear to see her standing by the window, ready to leap behind the curtain if any of the Banks's appear or to dash out if my darling sister deigns to show her face. All her hankies are in the wash, screwed up and wet because she's been continually running them through her fingers and crying.

God knows how she's going to cope with work tomorrow. She's a complete wreck!

I've been trying to put on a brave face. We've *got* to stick together and show the world we've got nothing to be ashamed of. I made myself go to The Trading Post yesterday. Opening the front door felt as if I was pushing against a giant wind that was trying to keep me in.

One part of me wanted to give up and leave it for another day. We didn't need anything desperately urgently. Only I knew if I left it even half an hour, it would be twice as hard.

I told myself it wouldn't be that bad. That I'd been building up all the stares and the whispers in my mind. Who did I think I was kidding? It took me five minutes to get from our house to the Parade. In that time, I met three neighbours – not ones that I know particularly well. One lot crossed over to avoid me, jerking this poor little kid in a push-chair right into the road. Another woman completely ignored me and the third – this bloke I've never even said hello to before – came up and wanted to know all the gory details. At first, I thought it was because he was sympathetic. What a joke! He asked me if it was true I was a lesbian. I said, yes. So what?

'*Oh, you don't look like one of them*'.

Ron Dixon wasn't exactly pleased to see me either. He kept his eyes well peeled while I went round the shelves. Did he think I was going to nick anything? That was Rachel's bad habit. Did he think I was going to leap on him and stick a knife in his back? What's he got to worry about? It wasn't him who beat and raped me.

Mike wasn't around, unfortunately. I didn't quite have the nerve to ask where he was. Just put my stuff on the counter and paid up. He didn't say a word to me, not even to say how much I owed.

When I left, I could almost hear the sigh of relief behind me.

21 February, 1995

Back to med. school today. Mum didn't want me to go. After having our names in the papers and on TV, she's scared to death of facing the big, wide world. The price of fame! It's precisely because of all the publicity that we've got to get back to normal. She can't just bury her head and wait until the trial comes up.

Sinbad and I gave her a long pep talk. We had to get her moving. She's always like this. If we let her, she'd just hide away for ever. Besides, she may have to find another job. They might not have kept her post open.

Today was a good day to start. It's half-term – Mum wanted to wait until the schools are back, but that's just putting off the evil day again. Sinbad promised he'd make her go to school.

What would I do without him? Crack up completely! He takes everything Mum throws at him. She even makes him kip in the extension, in case Rachel comes back and doesn't like them sleeping together. How's he supposed to know where he stands with her? He took me to one side this morning and asked me if I thought he ought to move back to the flat he rents in the Parade. Who else would even bother to ask? This *is* his house, after all. Anyway, I want him here. With Mum. He's going to give notice on the flat as soon as possible.

Uni was dreadful. People I thought I knew completely ignored me and people I've no desire to know went out of their way to ask me all sorts of questions. Viv was there. We smiled at each other, then this other girl came and sort of stood next to her. Protective. I shouldn't be surprised or hurt – especially since it was me that finished with her – but I was. Part of me sort of hoped she'd battle through all my objections, like Sinbad does with Mum. Stupid, really. We'd only known each other five minutes. There wasn't a whole history between us.

I survived the first lecture. Anatomy – my worst subject. The bloke who's taken over from Chris isn't a patch on her. I couldn't take in a word he was saying. It probably wasn't his fault, though. The state I was in, I wouldn't have heard someone telling me I'd won the Lottery.

I bet Chris would have supported me.

No. Get that right out of your mind, Beth. She didn't care. You were just a notch on her bedpost. At the first sign of trouble, she was off.

As I was on my way to the library, my tutor caught me. He asked for A Word. Which always means trouble. Even worse, he closed his office door behind me and offered me a coffee. Definitely hell was about to break loose!

It was put to me that it might be better if I took a year out. There were ample grounds and I could easily continue my studies – should all go well – next year. It would be such a pity if my current – ah – difficulties meant I couldn't achieve my full potential. The university was, of course, fully supportive, but under the circumstances, did I not think. . . .?

No! I did not think!! There's no way I'm doing that.

No way I'm going to hide and apologize and cringe. I want the world to know Trevor Jordache was killed because he was a nasty, evil, sadistic man. Then they can stop pointing the finger and talking about us.

He looked over the top of his glasses and said if that was the way I felt about it, fair enough. He must reiterate that in his opinion, it was not in my best interests, but it was, after all, my decision. If I should change my mind, his door is always open. Then he opened it, and I went out into the stares and avoidances of this fully supportive university.

22 February, 1995

Day 2 was even worse than Day 1! Every time I walk down the corridor, I can hear constant whispers behind my back. People who are supposed to be intelligent keep making stupid remarks and wanting to buy me drinks so they can say they've talked to a murderer.

My tutor sent for me again. This time, the powers-that-be had suggested I take time off until after the trial. I would be provided with the necessary course materials and tutorials. There should be no problem in my keeping up with the work at home, and it would surely make life easier if I didn't have to deal with the traumas that would inevitably result from others' – how should he put it – natural curiosity and judgements.

In other words, keep out of our university. Don't dirty our nice, clean reputation with your sordid story.

Tough. I'm going to go in every day that I have to. He's just going to have to accept it.

Mum, unfortunately, doesn't have the same choice. I came home to find her in tears and popping the paracetamol like there's no tomorrow. The school's suspended her on full pay until after the trial. Don't they understand that's the worst thing they could have done? She needs to get out of this place. Mum won't fight it. I know she's actually quite relieved she doesn't have to make the choice. There's no point in pushing it. They'd only sack her if she insisted on going in.

Yet another ordeal to go through – my first night back at Grants. Barry nodded at me and said 'glad to see you back', as though I'd been off sick for a few days. I never thought I'd be so grateful for someone treating me like a human being.

Emma was a bit funny, at first. I think she was just surprised to see me, though. When she got over the shock, she said, 'welcome back'. Then she started going on about her problems with Barry. He's trying to make her jealous by flirting with some other girl. She's trying to ignore it, but is deeply wounded. It was wonderful to talk about something other than the murder.

23 February, 1995

YOU BITCH
PERVERTS LIKE YOU DESERVE TO DIE
I HOPE YOU ROT IN HELL

That disgusting, sick note was delivered to our house this morning. Not signed, of course. How can people do that kind of thing? How can they sink so low? We're trying our best to get back to normal, then some creep has to send filth like that.

I didn't dare tell Mum. It'd finish her. She hasn't set foot outside the house since we got back. At this rate, she's going to get agoraphobic. All she does is stand at the window. Rachel went past this morning with Lee. She saw Mum and deliberately turned away. Mum was completely floored. People are talking about us enough already. It only makes matters worse when they see we're here and Rachel's still next door.

The trouble is, she's given in. As long as she can hide indoors she's all right. Every time I try to get her to go out, she puts me off with some stupid excuse. Maybe when Rachel comes home, is the latest one. It's so ridiculous. We all know how stubborn Rachel can be. It might be weeks before she changes her mind. Mum will just have to wait.

If only she'd make the effort. Go to the shops or the library, like she used to. Sinbad and I decided we aren't going to do any more shopping. If Mum won't go out, we'll just have to starve.

24 February, 1995

I had the day off college today. It was quite a relief to work at home. Not that I'd admit that to anyone. Mum ran out of flour and after a lot of persuading, I finally managed to force her out of the house.

We didn't get very far, Rosie Banks caught us up before we'd even reached the end of the path. She wanted to know what we're going to do about Rachel. Apparently, putting her up is causing trouble round at their place. I'm not surprised. Rosie wanted us to have another go at talking to her. Mum completely lost her nerve. She went absolutely white and darted back into the house like a frightened rabbit.

I felt quite sorry for Rosie. How was she to know Mum would react like that? The trouble is, we still need to do something about Rachel. Rosie agreed to let her stay for another few days. Reluctantly. This situation can't carry on much longer.

Even though Rosie was nice about it, the whole episode left me shaking. I didn't dare go back inside. If I give in once, that's it, I'm sure. Ron Dixon gave me this 'you're not welcome here' look when I went in. There was this stupid bloke at the counter, staring at me. He put me off so much I could hardly tell the difference between plain and self-raising. He and Ron were having a right old gossip.

'Is that the girl? The one that did It?'

Did they think I was deaf or something? That the papers are right? That we're murdering lesbians? I really lost my rag. I'm sick to death of people talking about me and Mum behind our backs. I saw red. Blood red dots were literally thumping up and down in front of my eyes. I told him to keep out of our business and slammed the bag of flour down on the counter. It was like a snow storm. Flour went everywhere. All over the till and the sweets and the newspapers. And over Ron Dixon.

He virtually threw me out. Said I was putting his customers off and that he didn't want me in there if I was going to kick off like that. I've never been so embarrassed in my life. Why can't I keep my cool? As soon as I'd opened my mouth, I knew I should have kept quiet. Luckily, Mike chose that moment to come in, so his Dad didn't say much more.

After everything that'd happened, I couldn't face going for a walk with Mike, so I went home. What else could go wrong, I thought?

Another poison pen letter! Hand-delivered to Mum this time. I tried to stop her from seeing it, pretending it was a circular, but she insisted on opening it.

It was as bad as the last one. Called Mum an evil witch, who deserved to die.

THEY SHOULD BRING BACK HANGING ESPECIALLY FOR YOU.

It was the same person who sent the one yesterday. I recognized the handwriting and the colour of the ink was the same.

Mum got completely hysterical. It's like whoever's doing this is getting closer. First, one comes through the post, then another is hand-delivered. Maybe there's someone out there watching us and waiting. They know us, but we don't know them.

I tried to calm her down and persuade her it's just

some stupid nutcase, with nothing better to do. They probably scan the newspapers every day to find someone to send them to. We must be an easy target.

Mum was OK after a while. It's really doing my head in, though. What kind of sick, perverted person would send something like that? What if it's someone from around here? What if they get into the house? I daren't show Mum how worried I am, but I'll crack up if we get much more of this.

God knows how I got myself upstairs to bed tonight. I buried my head in the pillow and cried and cried and cried.

25 February, 1995

I hardly slept a wink last night. I look like death. My skin's breaking out, I've lost weight. Everything tastes like sawdust. I don't know how long I can keep going. It just doesn't let up for a minute. Even at the restaurant tonight, there were people whispering. Emma and Barry are the only ones who'll talk to me. Everyone else acts as though I'm going to grab a meat cleaver and hack them to pieces if they so much as look at me. Max Farnham's the worst. He's supposed to be the boss, but he acts like a worm. Whenever I come into the room, he backs away, like he's trying to get up against a wall for protection. I know he's dying for me to take time off sick or something. Luckily, he daren't say anything with Barry around.

Mum's in an even worse state. She can't think about anything except the trial, what the neighbours are saying, and how to get Rachel home. The only way she can have even the remotest form of contact is to talk to Eddie and Rosie Banks. She got Eddie to ask one of Rachel's friends to have a word with her. It's so humiliating for her. How can Rachel put her own mother through all this? Part of me's dreading her coming home. She'll make our lives even more hellish than they are already.

Not that we'll have to worry about that at the moment. We got the report back quick enough. Rachel said she'd sooner go into a kids' home than live here with us.

26 February, 1995

Mike came round today for a chat. We spent most of the time talking about his latest disaster, which was a great relief. He's got a new girlfriend and she's got a kid and it's all hassle. Actually, it really cheered me up, listening to completely normal, ordinary problems.

Mum came in looking like a prophet of doom. She really gets on my nerves sometimes. Here's me and Sinbad doing the best we can, yet she won't do a thing to help herself. Mike said hello and asked how she was and that. All Mum could say was that she'd been better. The atmosphere was terrible. It was obvious she couldn't wait for him to go, so off he went. Then she had the cheek to moan on that wherever she goes, people make their excuses and leave – even in her own house. It might help if she made them feel a bit more welcome.

There was another letter for her today. I tore it up without reading it and before Mum had a chance to see it. The last thing she needs at the moment is hate mail. She hates herself enough as it is.

28 February, 1995

I've never seen Mum so determined in her life. Rachel pushed and pushed and pushed until she couldn't stand it any longer. Mum tried to talk to her over the back fence for about the hundredth time. Yet again, Rachel turned her back, leaving Mum standing in front of the Banks, completely humiliated.

'That's it, I've had enough,' Mum said. 'I'm going next door. I'm going to bring my daughter home'.

She marched through the house and out the front door. You could hear her hammering next door right down the street. This from the woman who normally cowers if anyone so much as glances at her! I waited in the living-room. Given how much Rachel detests me at the moment, I reckoned I'd only make things worse if I interfered.

A few minutes later Mum was back, angrier than I've ever seen her before. She'd found Rachel tossing pancakes with the Banks. We'd completely forgotten it was

Shrove Tuesday. Mum told Rachel quietly, but firmly to come home. Rachel went completely wild. She started screaming and shouting, throwing frying pans and pancake batter and God knows what all over the floor. Mum, Rosie, Eddie and Carl all tried to reason with her, but it was no use. Rachel dashed up the stairs to escape Mum's clutches and locked herself in the bathroom.

At which point Mum came back to fetch me. Reinforcements! We then spent the next hour and a half pleading, threatening and cajoling outside the bathroom door. Personally, I'd had enough of the softly, softly approach. Rachel was being completely unreasonable and the way she's been treating Mum just makes me see red. Mum was in a right state, embarrassed at this scene happening in front of the neighbours and stressed out by all the horrible things Rachel was shouting at her. I wouldn't mind betting she was furious underneath it all, as well. You could tell Rosie was fast getting to the end of her tether. She's had enough to put up with, what with the press camping outside the door and then having Rachel to stay.

In the meantime, Eddie and Carl were having the most ridiculous conversation. If the situation hadn't been so fraught, it would have been funny. Not a lot of father/son bonding going on between those two!

'You were in the army. Didn't they give you hostage training or something?' Eddie said.

'Yeah', Carl replied. 'Stun grenade through the window then kick the door down'.

Which sounded good to me, but Eddie told him not to be daft.

Then Carl had another idea.

'It's only a mickey mouse lock', he said. 'If I was to put me shoulder against the door . . .'

'Don't be daft, lad. You've been watching too much Starsky and Hutch'.

'What if I got a screwdriver and took the hinges off?'

'The hinges are on the inside, soft lad'. Eddie wasn't about to take any of Carl's suggestions seriously.

'Alright, you think of something'.

At which point, Rosie lost her rag. Until then, she'd been calm and reasonable – through gritted teeth. I think her husband and son acting like complete prats did it.

'Let's just do whatever', she shouted. 'Let's get this sorted. Get this Rachel back home. Look, I'm sorry, Mandy, but this carry-on has gone on long enough. She's just going to have to go.'

Everyone shut up. There was a long, long pause, then the bathroom door opened. Rachel came out, completely calm and looking like she hated the whole world.

'So you don't want me either', she said to Rosie. 'Nobody wants me. I hate you all'.

I grabbed her before she could lock herself in again. Mum and I literally had to drag her down the stairs and back next door. The Crosbies and the Farnhams had to choose that moment to emerge, of course. Rachel was making a right scene, struggling to get away and screaming her head off about murderers, lesbians and kidnappers. Jean Crosbie came running over, but the last thing we needed was her interfering. Luckily, we got inside before she could catch us up.

Rachel had another go at us.

'You don't want me. Nobody does. Poor, poor me!'

Given the way she's been behaving, it's hardly surprising, but Mum takes it all in. I wish she'd give up – it only upsets her. There's no point in reasoning with Rachel in this mood.

Eventually, Rachel shut herself in her room. Mum left it for a while before taking a sandwich up to her. Rachel opened the door just enough to be able to knock the plate out of Mum's hand, then she slammed it in her face again. As a final piece of nastiness, she turned her radio on full blast. Along with everything else, we've got to endure 24-hours' non-stop assault on our ears.

1 March, 1995

I'm not sure how much longer I can stand being here. Rachel kept the noise up continuously until this afternoon. It was driving us all crazy. Mum wanted to crouch outside her door and plead. No way were Sinbad and I going to let her do that!

After I left for college this morning, Sinbad started redecorating the living room. Mum always said she hated the wallpaper. Of course, she thought there was no point, seeing as how she's going to prison, etc., etc. Undaunted, Chamois Man was in there with his scraper, ignoring her feeble cries and getting on with his life. Exactly what we've all got to do – including Mum. Why can't she be positive for once?

As soon as the music stopped, Mum wanted to go straight up and talk to Rachel. Sinbad wouldn't let her. Best to let her come down by herself when she's good and hungry, he said. Quite. Apparently, it didn't take long.

Then Mum had to go and overdo things again. She'd made a cottage pie and tried to coax Rachel into eating some, even though she'd only gone into the kitchen for toast. Can't she see that Rachel won't accept anything from any of us at the moment? The result was that Rachel made another of her offensive little speeches and went back to her room without anything.

Later on, Mum got an anonymous phone call. First, there was silence. Then some sicko started calling Mum every name under the sun, saying she was evil and a murdering bitch. When I got back from uni, hours later, Mum was still shaking on the sofa.

What kind of a person could do something like that? Somebody in urgent need of treatment, to say the least. I bet it's the same one who's been sending the hate mail. It sounds like the same kind of mind to me.

2 March, 1995

Rachel and I had a huge row this morning. She came downstairs for breakfast, but refused to let Mum make it for her. I told her to stop being so rude and upsetting Mum.

'So what?' she said. 'I'm upset as well, but nobody cares about me'.

We've done nothing else but care for her for weeks. Care about her, talk about her, plan for her home-coming. It's not as if we haven't got a hell of a lot of other things on our minds!

Rachel completely lost it. We had another full-blown temper tantrum.

'If you cared about me, you wouldn't have made me come back here. Forced me to live with her. I don't want to live in the same house as a lesbian'.

When I tried to interrupt, she really went for me.

'I bet it was your idea to kill my Dad. What are you going to do? Kill me as well? Bury me under the patio? I hate you and I'd rather live in some horrible kids' home than stay here with you'.

I can't stand much more of this. Neither can Mum. After all she's been through, she doesn't deserve this. I went for a walk in Sefton Park this afternoon to clear my head and decide what to do.

One thing's clear, Rachel's never going to calm down while I'm in the house. No amount of discussion will change her mind. It's completely closed. She's not prepared to budge an inch.

Poor Mum's an absolute wreck. Keeping Rachel at home is desperately important to her, but the way things are going, she'll run off back to London if we're not careful. There's only one thing for it. I'm going to have to move out — at least for a while. Mum and Rachel need a bit of space to sort things out between them. I hate the thought of leaving Mum. She'll be alright with Sinbad to look after her. But who's going to look after me?

3 March, 1995

It's not exactly easy to find a place right in the middle of the academic year. Every single cheap room and most of the expensive ones are already over-occupied. The student union didn't have anything. The best they could do was put me on the list for priority housing.

As for my so-called friends, they've disappeared into the hills. Dead sorry and all that, but there's no room. The landlady wouldn't approve. I bet! Who'd want a murdering lesbian sharing the bathroom?

I even thought about asking Viv. I saw her in the common room this afternoon, chatting with the woman I saw her with before. When I went over, Viv looked up and smiled. I'm sure she'd've been all right, only her new girlfriend muttered something about them being late and dragged her away. No chance there!

My tutor — the one who's door is always open —

wasn't any help. Oh, he was dead sympathetic. Completely useless, but he did it in an understanding way. He doesn't have access to any accommodation suitable for an undergraduate. Can't even arrange a bit of floor-space with a psychology professor who might like an interesting subject to study.

Things were a bit calmer at home. Rachel spent the evening in her bedroom. Until I can find somewhere else, we'll have to act like those 'wet and fine' wooden dolls you get in clocks. When one goes out, the other has to come in.

Mum was looking a bit happier. Jean Crosbie came round for a cup of tea. Apparently, she's totally supportive and on our side. They had a good long natter in the kitchen. Jean actually saw what Dad was like. She and David Crosbie came round for Mum and Dad's anniversary last year. I remember Mum telling me what an awful occasion it was. Dad watched every move she made, with that horrible false jollity he used to put on. As the evening went on, he got more and more drunk and started criticizing Mum and putting her down. Jean and David left them to it as quickly as possible. Dad was furious and blamed Mum for them leaving so early and for no other guests turning up. The next day Mum was covered in bruises.

Jean told Mum that she really regretted not doing anything about it then. That must happen so often. People know these things go on, but they don't do anything about it. Not that it's really Jean's fault. What could she have done? Gone to the police? Dad would have killed us all, for sure, if she'd done that.

No. We were completely and utterly trapped. As Jean said herself, what Mum did was self-defence. There was no other way out.

4 March, 1995

Rosie Banks was 40 today. There was a big party next door, to which we were invited – reluctantly. We were supposed to turn the invitation down. It was quite funny in a way. Rosie came to the back door in that slightly awkward way she has.

'Erm – we're having a bit of a do this evening. Me fortieth. It'll be a bit noisy. Just thought I'd warn you. You're welcome to pop in, of course. Only we'll quite understand if you don't feel up to it, like'.

Eddie Banks' face was a picture when I walked in. Gobsmacked or what! Naturally, I was on my own. Mum couldn't face it and Rachel was sulking in her room. All the neighbours were there. One or two came up to me, said a couple of words, then hurried off to the buffet. Nothing special, but it meant they were talking to me.

Ron Dixon and his new bit, Bev, gave me the cold shoulder. No surprise there! I heard Bev whispering something about me having the nerve to show my face. Why shouldn't I? We've got nothing to hide.

I got a drink and looked around for someone to stand next to. Everyone turned away as soon as I caught their eye. Then Mike came in. Rescue, at last. It was really good to talk to him. After all that's happened, he's still prepared to stand by me. I told him I didn't care what people said. It sort of made it true.

He was understanding about my housing problem. He even said he'd ask his Dad, only they're a bit over-crowded at the moment. I can just see Ron Dixon welcoming me with open arms! Mike did have a more hopeful suggestion. Jacqui and Katie have let him stay before now, so he said he'd have a word with them. I promised it would only be for a couple of weeks. It would be great to be so near Mum. Just in case something happened.

Trust the Jordache family to provide the cabaret. I went into the kitchen to get another drink and who should I find there? Rachel. Sneaking cider to get sloshed with her mates. I might have known. I ordered her to put it down, but she won't take any notice of what I say. Then Mum appeared. Very quietly, she told Rachel it was time to go home.

Immediately, Rachel went off into one of her scenes. She actually dared to tell her own mother to get lost. I tried to calm her down. It was so embarrassing – her showing herself up like that. She just doesn't give a damn any more.

'Frightened I'll ruin the family name, are you?' she shrieked. 'Murderers, lesbians and thieves? Well, that's what we are. Keep your husbands away from these two, everybody. Because they'll kill them. Man-haters and murderers. They're going to lock you up, you know. You're both going away for ever'.

She spat the words out like venom. Of course, every single guest had crowded into the kitchen to see what was going on. Mum looked as though she was about to faint. I wanted to sink through the floor. We bundled Rachel out of there as fast as we could.

Back home, Rachel escaped to her room, leaving Mum and me completely shattered. Tomorrow, I'm going to tell Mum I'm going away for a while. Even if Jacqui and Katie won't have me, I can't stay here another day.

5 March, 1995

I won't have to face Rachel's sulks and hysterics for a while, but I'm not sure if it isn't out of the frying pan into the blazing furnace.

Mike and I went round to Jacqui and Katie's first thing this morning. He had to do a lot of persuading before they'd let me stay. I waited downstairs. It was awful. The shop directly under the flat used to be a hairdresser's. Very classy, but it turned out the owner was a drug-pusher. He was arrested a few months back and the place closed down.

Funny the things that run through your mind while your entire future's being decided for you. I kept thinking what a good thing it'd be for someone to reopen the salon. There's probably a load of money to be made from it.

The only place to hang around was in the corridor at

the back of the shop. I waited for half an hour, not quite able to hear what was going on and not daring to go any closer to listen in. You could've heard footsteps a mile off in that place.

At long last, Mike came down with a sheepish grin on his face. They'd said yes, but reluctantly. I followed him back upstairs. Jacqui and Katie were standing in the middle of the living-room like a sort of reception committee. I felt a bit like a refugee from World War Two. All I needed was a luggage label round my neck and a gas mask. The two girls were clutching cups of coffee with both hands for protection. Mike ducked out as quickly as he could and left us to it.

I'm pretty sure it's Jacqui who was iffy about me staying. She's too like her Dad for comfort, i.e., full of stupid prejudices. Katie's much quieter and she actually deigned to smile at me. I get the feeling that mostly what Jacqui says goes. We spent the evening in front of the telly, not saying much. Katie looked like she wanted to be friendly. A couple of times she looked my way, then Jacqui would shift in her chair or cough or something and the moment would pass.

At one point, Jacqui got up to make herself a coffee. She offered Katie one, but not me.

'I expect Beth'd like one as well', Katie said, so Jacqui had to play hostess. It was kind of Katie, but I wish she hadn't bothered. Jacqui didn't say another word to me all evening.

Before I settled down on the sofa, I nipped out to ring Mum. The atmosphere was too frosty for me to ask to use the phone in the flat. Mum wouldn't speak properly, even though Rachel was safely tucked away upstairs. It was almost impossible to hear her mumbling in the receiver. She and Sinbad are OK and apparently Rachel came down for a few minutes once I'd gone. I suppose the sacrifice is worth it.

6 March, 1995

I've never spent a lonelier night in my life. Even though Mum and Sinbad are only five minutes' walk away, it feels like they're in another hemisphere. They've got each other and Jean's been round a couple of times. Who can I turn to? My own home is out of bounds, because my sister can't stand the sight of me. Mike would be supportive, but after what happened at New Year, I'm terrified to let him get any closer to me. My so-called mates at uni have turned their backs, my tutor's doing his best to get me out, and the flat's so tense the plates threaten to jump off the draining-board every second.

Be positive. Smile. Show them you don't care.

The couch is comfy enough, but I couldn't sleep. Everything seems so much more depressing in the dark. I didn't dare cry in case I woke the others. A cup of tea would have gone down a treat, but that would have been noisy. Instead, I just lay there, not moving a muscle, getting cramp in my leg. It was four o'clock before I plucked up the nerve to go to the loo.

Breakfast was a nightmare. I waited until Jacqui was in the bathroom before I even attempted to get some. Without saying anything, she managed to make it clear I was in the way. Overcrowded AND lonely – what a way to exist!

Jacqui got off early. She's a lifeguard at the leisure centre and Katie's studying dance, so she can have more of a lie-in. Once Jacqui was out of the way, it got more relaxed. Katie was still a bit awkward, but at least she was talking to me.

People do have some funny ideas about lesbians. There were some sausages in the fridge for breakfast. Katie thought I wouldn't eat them because I was gay. Obviously, it meant I must be a veggie as well! Still, it could have been a lot worse. God knows what stupid assumptions Jacqui's made about me. Katie also wanted to know about the trial. When would it be? Were the papers telling the truth? and, of course, how did we do it?

I think I'd probably have told her if Jacqui hadn't come back at that moment. I'm NOT discussing my private life with her. It's different with Katie. I get the impression she's mostly curious because I've been dumped on her. Plus the fact that she's naturally quite a sympathetic person.

Since I've only got lectures in the morning, I decided to go back to the flat after lunch. I couldn't face working in the faculty library. Unfortunately, Jacqui's shift had finished – and she was obviously not chuffed to have me invading her space! I offered to help her with the cleaning, seeing I'd got the afternoon off. You'd've thought I'd made a pass at her from her reaction. What's she so scared of? That my dirty lesbian tendencies will rub off on the furniture?

She's got this phrase she uses all the time – *I'm not being funny, but* . . . Of course, it means she *is* about to be funny about something . . . How long did I think I'll be staying? I said I'd be out of the way as soon as possible.

I meant it!!

7 March, 1995

I overheard Jacqui warning Katie against me this morning. Where on earth did she hear such a load of rubbish about lesbians? From what I could gather, Jacqui's got it into her head that I fancy Katie. She wanted to wait for her in case I came up and grabbed her. The trouble is, Jacqui's prejudices are making Katie terrified to be in the same room as me.

I really fancied a swim today, only the uni pool's shut for repairs. Katie said the leisure centre's got one, but warned me that Jacqui would be on duty this afternoon. I decided it would be a good opportunity to have a word with her. It's obviously a pain for them having me here, but I've nowhere else to go. It would be better if we could be friends. We may as well get on if we're going to live in each other's pockets.

Jacqui didn't look exactly pleased to see me. I stood

at the poolside, shivering in my costume, while she swanned about in her dinky little uniform, blowing her whistle every five seconds. Maybe I shouldn't have got changed, but I didn't want it to look as if I'd planned to have a word with her.

Why did I bother? She's not remotely interested in getting on with me. I couldn't even get her to look me in the eye, let alone take a couple of minutes out for a chat. She just muttered something about being on duty and scurried off to give some poor kid a hard time for dive-bombing her brother.

Afterwards, it occurred to me that she might have been embarrassed because she was at work, but it wasn't any better back at the flat. She glued herself in front of the TV and went off to bed at 10.00 pm.

10 March, 1995

How can people do this to us? What kind of evil, sadistic mind could sit down and cut letters out of a newspaper, glue them into an evil message and send them to a perfect stranger? Or even worse, to someone they know? This latest letter was complete filth. Hysterical. Accusing me of all sorts of things.

When I saw the envelope, I knew what it was immediately. Same writing, same ink as before. Is someone getting a kick out of this? The picture keeps running through my mind of some evil pervert getting turned on at the thought of me in tears. All day long,

I've been acting like a zombie. Eating's impossible. So's reading, listening to the radio, watching TV. Everything. Every time I've tried to do something constructive, those disgusting words leap up in front of my eyes.

Katie caught me crying. I couldn't help it. She was really sweet. She put her arm round me while I sobbed my heart out. When I'd calmed down, she put the kettle on. I'm glad it was her, not Jacqui. I dread to think what her reaction would've been.

There's nowhere I can be private here. If I stay in the bathroom for more than two seconds, Jacqui comes knocking on the door, wanting to know how long I'm going to be. I can't even retreat to bed until the others are ready to switch the telly off. I can't stand this much longer – I've got to find somewhere else. SOON!!!

14 March, 1995

Jacqui chucked me out! Not exactly surprising, but I could've done with a couple more days to sort myself out. Under the circumstances, she could have been a lot worse. She said she was sorry (what a liar!), but there wasn't enough room and she'd only offered because Mike asked her and it wasn't as though I was really a mate of theirs, etc., etc., etc. Everything except the truth – which is that she can't cope with having a murdering lesbian under her roof.

There was no point in arguing. I packed my bags and

went. Thank goodness for my uni friends who'll put me up.

I popped back home while Rachel was at school. Mum was looking a lot better. There weren't quite so many bags under her eyes and her jumper wasn't as pulled out of shape. While Sinbad was out on his round, we had a good long natter.

On the down side, she's still getting stick from a lot of the neighbours. Mr. Dixon's Bev crosses the street every time she sees her. Not much of a loss, in my opinion. Also, Mum got another bit of hate mail yesterday. Sinbad chucked it in the bin before she could read it properly, but it still upset her a lot. I didn't tell her about the one I got. She's got enough to worry about.

On the up side, it looks like Rachel's calming down a bit. She's giving Mum an incredibly hard time, but at least they're speaking. Jean's been round and the Banks are still friendly – in spite of all the commotion about Rachel. It's good to know there's a few people on our side.

Mum's main worry was me! As if I can't look after myself!! Now I've got somewhere to stay, I'll be fine. I promised I'd ring every day, when Rachel's not around.

17 March, 1995

I'm frightened. Really scared. The latest poison pen letter was in my pigeon hole at uni. Whoever's doing this is getting nearer. It can't be some stranger picking my name out of the tabloids. How did they know my middle name's Ann or what my date of birth is? None of that stuff was in the papers. Someone really close to me and Mum is behind it. There's no other explanation.

I didn't mean to tell Mum, but I was too scared to stay by myself. It was such a relief to sit on our own settee, drinking from my favourite mug. Mum wasn't looking too brilliant. She's been sick a couple of times and feels generally under the weather. Apparently, there may be a bug going around, which could be serious. I think most of the problem's that she's worried she's got it.

Next week, Mum and I have an appointment to see our solicitor. Her name's Alison Dicks and she specializes in domestic violence cases. With all the publicity, it'd be a good one to pick up. *Cause célèbre* and all that.

25 March, 1995

Something weird's happening at Brookside. We couldn't see this Alison Dicks, because Mum's been quarantined. The whole of the Close and the Parade have been cordoned off. That bug going around has turned into a deadly epidemic. Two people have died already – one of them was a mate of Rachel's.

I can't believe it's happening! My mind won't take it in. I should be feeling completely awful that somebody younger than me is actually dead. Somehow, it doesn't seem real. There's been stuff about it in the papers, but it's happening to other people, somewhere else.

Mum nearly had hysterics when I suggested going round, so I haven't been near. Sinbad told me there's a barrier up at the edge of the Close. No-one can come in, no-one can go out. The members of the gallant Brookside Residents Association take it in turns to guard it.

All except David Crosbie. Jean's really ill and he hardly leaves her bedside for a moment. They think she might die.

On the surface, Jean comes across as an ordinary OAP, nice enough and a saint (or a martyr) to put up with Bing. Yet there's so much more to her than that. She really thinks about things. What I like best about her is how brave she is. It took a lot of guts for her to stand up for me and Mum when everyone else had been giving us the cold shoulder. And she won't stand for any of Mr. Crosbie's intolerant attitudes.

Patricia Farnham's the only one who's allowed to cross the cordon. Her son, Thomas, caught the virus and was rushed to hospital. Max is away in Florida on a business trip. Trust him to be out of touch when he's really needed.

The one good thing about this epidemic is that the post can't get through. Mum doesn't have to face any more hate mail for the moment.

26 March, 1995

Mother's Day. I sent Mum a card, but she won't get it until this cordon is lifted. The powers-that-be are treating the whole thing really seriously. People who happened to be in the area at the time are having to doss down with residents. No-one's allowed to go to work and the kids are off school. Not that they mind!

There's a mobile medical unit parked in the Close. Everyone has to give blood and urine samples.

Mum's still been feeling under the weather and I know she and Sinbad were both a bit worried she might have it. The funny thing was, when I called her today, she sounded really happy. I haven't heard her giggle like that for ages. We had this peculiar conversation, where she went on about such a surprise and at her age and how wonderful everything was.

All I wanted to know was what the hell was going on. It was only when Sinbad got on the line that I could get a sensible answer. Even then it took five minutes to spit it out.

MUM'S PREGNANT!!!!!

Chamois Man and my mother having a baby! I can't get over it. By Christmas, we'll be knee-deep in nappies. I'll have a brother or another sister.

At first, I couldn't tell whether I was delighted or horrified. A bit of both probably. Mum said she was the same. Especially with the trial coming up. I said 'Congratulations' and put the phone down in a complete daze.

Five minutes later, I phoned back and we had a proper conversation. Mum had no idea she'd conceived. Apparently, with everything else going on, they hadn't even considered contraception. The stick the younger generation gets about taking responsibility and my own mother doesn't even think about it!

Still, once I'd had a chance to get over the shock, I realized it was the best possible thing that could have happened to her. Sinbad is over the moon. He's longing to be a Dad and I know he'll be a good one. If the worst comes to the worst, he'll stick by Mum and the baby and make sure they're both looked after.

28 March, 1995

Carl Banks is allowed through the cordon, because he's had this 'plague' and survived. The good news is that he can bring in supplies. The bad news is he can also fetch the post. Mum got my Mother's Day card — and two more pieces of hate mail.

It's really odd. They're definitely from the same person, but they've been posted in different places. One of these came from Warrington and the other from Bolton. It must be from somebody who travels a lot. Who do we know that's a long-distance lorry driver? Or maybe it's some travelling salesman.

I haven't had any more for a few days. Unless Mum and Sinbad aren't passing them on.

We should throw them in the bin without even reading them. They don't deserve that. Getting all upset is playing right into this maniac's hands.

But it's impossible! There's something about a letter that makes you open it. Every time, I think there may be a clue as to who's doing it. How am I supposed to keep going – be positive – get on with my life with someone knocking me down every chance they get?

29 March, 1995

Mum was in a total state when I rang this evening. She'd forgotten Rachel's birthday. Sixteen today! I remembered, but didn't send a card. The way Rachel's been reacting towards me lately, I don't think it would have gone down too well.

Of course, Rachel used it as an excuse to make Mum feel completely awful. She's such a cow. Never misses an opportunity! Mum told me exactly what she said.

'I know how low I come on your list of priorities. I'm used to Beth being the one-and-only. I know you never loved me, Mum. Fair enough, I don't care, but I'm sixteen now, so I can go whenever I want'.

The trouble is, there's an element of truth in it. I've had to be extra-close to Mum to look after her. She relied on me all those years. Still does – in spite of Sinbad. We banded together to protect ourselves and to protect Rachel. Why can't she see that? She's got no time for anybody's feelings except her own. OK, she's gone through a hell of a lot. So have the rest of us.

The one thing – the big thing – I can't understand is why she keeps up this pretence of Dad being the perfect father. She saw what went on. All those evenings when she was little, crouched on the landing, listening to Dad shouting at Mum. There would be a terrible lull, when we couldn't hear anything. Then the thumps and the muffled screams as he beat the living daylights out of her.

How could Rachel possibly have forgotten all that?

31 March, 1995

We're in the papers again. This time it seems we're the cause of the plague!

> '*Some local residents, however, believe the source of the infection can be directly traced to no. 10, the notorious house of death, where the corpse of Trevor Jordache was discovered under the patio. His wife, Amanda Jordache, 39, with the help of her student daughter, Elizabeth, 19, a self-confessed lesbian, is accused of fatally stabbing him*'.

It's so ridiculous, it's almost comic. Mum's worried about what Rachel will think if she sees that load of rubbish. According to her, we're responsible for every-thing that's gone wrong in the world, so it's not going to surprise her that we're responsible for the virus as well.

Mum's really losing it. She told me that before she even mentioned the really important stuff.

SINBAD'S POPPED THE QUESTION!!

I *knew* it was only a matter of time. Mum should've leapt at the chance and dashed down to the registry office then and there. Of course, she didn't. Instead, she went on about maybe having to go to prison and she couldn't expect Sinbad to wait for her, etc., etc., etc. Typical! Anyone with half a brain can see that Sinbad will wait for her no matter what and for how-ever long it takes. When's she going to realize – Sinbad's one of the good guys.

3 April, 1995

Rachel's finally calming down. Everything seems to be OK. She still isn't talking to me, but she isn't flying off the handle either.

4 April, 1995

Mum decided we ought to do something for Rachel's

birthday. She wanted a tea party for the four of us – her, me, Sinbad and the birthday girl. Sinbad and I thought it would be better to have a proper party with a few guests.

I thought it would be a good opportunity to show people we're getting on with our lives. Besides, some of the neighbours have been really good to us. It would be a way of thanking them.

We've got nothing to be ashamed of, nothing to hide. Maybe we should charge an admission fee. Now that everyone knows, why not exploit the situation? Make some money out of it – like the tabloids. We could turn the place into a theme park.

The 'do' was all arranged for this afternoon. I telephoned Chantelle and some of her other mates. Sinbad rounded up the neighbours. He also laid on a bottle of bubbly!

Seeing how Rachel's been lately, I thought she'd feel more like the centre of attention if I wasn't around too much. So I stayed away, went to the multiplex and saw two movies.

Mum said it was quite a good turn-out. Jean came – having recovered from the Virus. The Banks were there, including Lee, and a few other neighbours. Three of Rachel's friends came, which was a bit disappointing. I must have called about a dozen of them. The Dixons and the Farnhams didn't show up.

Everything was going okay, Mum decided it would be a good time to tell Rachel about the baby. She called Rachel down and took her to one side.

Rachel went berserk. It was yet another of her awful scenes. She attacked Mum. Actually attacked her, grabbing her shoulders and pushing her hard against the unit.

The guests retreated to the kitchen, leaving Sinbad to tackle Rachel. It took all his strength to pull her off. All the time she was screaming about Mum being stupid and evil and the rest.

When Rachel had finished going for Mum, she started on the guests. She told them all to go – even Lee, who'd been transfixed on the stairs. He didn't have a clue what was going on. Her other mates faded away and the neighbours put their glasses down and ran.

The last to go was Jean. Rachel came in a few minutes later with an overnight bag. Jean invited her to stay at theirs. Rachel went with her, which was a huge relief to all of us. Otherwise, God knows where she'd've ended up.

She vowed never to set foot in this house again. What's the matter with her? Mum and Sinbad went out of their way to make things nice for her tonight and she throws it all right back in their faces. She's going from bad to worse. We're right back where we started.

When she'd gone, Mum just collapsed in tears on the sofa. There was nothing Sinbad could do.

Mum kept crying over and over again, 'She hates me. She really hates me'.

The awful thing is, it's true – Rachel loathes all of us.

7 April, 1995

Jean is a saint. It's official! Rachel's agreed to stay over there for a few weeks. Mum's so relieved. At least we know she's going to be properly looked after.

Everything Rachel does is designed to hurt Mum. The latest thing is that she's left school. Mum was horrified. She always wanted us both to get a good education. I know she's never been interested in studying like I have, but she's got a perfectly good brain. Why can't she see she's hurting herself far more than us by doing this?

Maybe when everything's calmed down, she'll change her mind. She *is* only sixteen – there's plenty of time yet. Besides, the Crosbies are the type who'd be dead keen on education. If she starts to trust them, maybe they can persuade her to take her GCSEs.

Jean reports in every day. I don't know what we'd do without her. I have to admit, even David Crosbie must have his good points to put up with my revolting little sister.

I found Mum looking very sheepish behind the net curtains this afternoon. She said a big part of her's relieved that Rachel's not here any more. Me too, but I'm not going to feel guilty about it and neither should Mum. We did our best. What else could we have done?

11 April, 1995

It's that time of year again! Revision!!! I've missed such a lot one way or another, I should be buried in my books, but it's going very slowly.

There are so many distractions. Mum haunts the living-room window, trying to catch a glimpse of Rachel. She worries the whole time. Will Rachel be alright at the Crosbies? What if she disappears down to London again?

I wish she wouldn't drag herself over the coals about it. What she should be concerned about is the baby. Rachel will be back in her own time and there's nothing we can do about it. With Jean to keep an eye on her, we can make sure she doesn't escape to the Great Metropolis.

Sinbad and I do our best to make Mum put her feet up. Expectant mothers need rest. Once the baby's here, she won't have a moment to herself.

What if she does? What if she has *every* moment to herself? Stuck in prison, away from Sinbad, away from the baby? Away from me – banged up in a different cell at the other end of the country?

I try and try to put it out of my mind, but sometimes when I'm persuading my eyes to focus on a text-book, it's like shadows of bars descend on the page and I can't read a thing. It's just my stupid imagination. If I'm going to keep sane, I've GOT to be positive. We all have.

Mum got another anonymous letter. I put it straight

in the bin, where it belongs. We knew it was there, though, sending out waves of evil like a stink bomb. Why won't they stop? If only I could find out who's behind it, I'd make them sorry they ever learned to write.

Sinbad's doing better than me in the positive thinking stakes. He suggested we turn the extension into a bedsit for Rachel. Sort of treating her like an adult. Mum wasn't convinced, but neither of us had a better idea. It might work.

As soon as he'd finished his round, Sinbad was down the DIY shop, stocking up on trendy pastels and borders for Rachel's room and this dead cute paper for the nursery. He's spending every minute he can decorating. It's just what we ALL need.

12 April, 1995

Mum and I had to go to see our solicitor today. We had to go through everything – what Dad used to be, the murder, the chase, what we said to the police. What we didn't say . . .

It didn't seem real, sitting there in Alison Dicks's posh office. She was completely calm while we told her our story. There's no question that she believes us. Every so often, when Mum came out with something particularly hideous that Dad did, Alison would purse her lips and frown a bit. I got the impression she was trying not to do that, to keep everything damped down.

On the bus, we chatted about the baby. Mum's already been for a check-up and everything's fine. For a moment, I was a bit surprised that she hadn't mentioned it before. Normally, there's be huge discussions about something like that. I suppose she had them with Sinbad. He *is* the baby's father after all. I'll only be his or her sister. Half-sister, to be precise.

Sinbad had a quiet word with me after supper. It seems Mum wasn't as all right as she'd seemed. He caught her in the half-finished nursery, sobbing into a roll of wallpaper.

I can't blame her. The thought of prison makes me turn cold. I could get life. Mum's even more likely to. Now, there's the thought of the baby being born inside. Sinbad will have to look after it, no matter what, but imagine having to go through nine months of pregnancy with that hanging over your head! No wonder it's doing Mum's head in.

Sinbad's almost promised to look after Rachel. She's really getting on at the Crosbies. Even Bing likes her, amazingly. Jean told us that he got all of Patricia's old things down from the loft. Rachel thought the old seventies stuff was hilarious, except for a pair of platform shoes. They're cool again – Jean and David think they're hideous.

Mum's really relieved she's doing so well across the road, but it's still depressing. Why can't she be like that with us?

13 April, 1995

Sinbad finished the decorating in record time. He's worked incredibly hard on it. The nursery's dead cute. It's a bit bare at the moment, but Sinbad's threatening to go shopping for every single cot, pram, buggy, mobile, potty and rattle he can lay his hands on. There won't be room for the baby!

The extension's completely transformed. Rachel will think she's in bedsitland. The walls are in this sort of maroon colour, with a patterned border about a third of the way up. We haven't got any money for new furniture, but it looks completely different in the extension. Spruced up and smart. Mum and I spent ages shifting all Rachel's things in there. It's a real home-from-home. I'm quite jealous!

There's probably no point in doing my room up, though. Alison Dicks called this afternoon. They've set the court date. The trial starts in three weeks.

8TH MAY 1995

We've got to go and see her again in a few days' time. When Mum told me, I started to panic. I had to go and hide in my room so she wouldn't see.

After all we've gone through, I'm not going to ruin it now. In three-weeks' time, we'll get our chance to tell the world the truth. If we plead self-defence, we're bound to get off.

15 April, 1995

Disaster! Rachel came back while the lovebirds were out shopping. Of course, she went straight up to her room, only to find it's turned into a nursery. She hit the roof! Mum and Sinbad came back in time to see her marching out with the rest of her clothes in a bin bag.

She wouldn't even look at the converted extension. Sinbad had to physically drag her into the room. She was far too gone to be impressed. As far as she's concerned, we've pushed her out to make room for the new baby. Nothing we say is ever going to change her mind.

Sinbad told her she'd always have a home with him, no matter what happens to Mum. Useless. She said she'd rather live with the Yorkshire Ripper than with him. Did we seriously expect her to stay in the house with Mum's boyfriend where they killed her precious father?

When I'd got over being furious with her, I suppose I could see what she meant a bit. It's like we're on opposite sides and there's no chance of a cease-fire or even peace talks.

Rachel's back at the Crosbies and the rest of us keep our eyes away from the extension door.

Mum got another poison pen letter. Posted in Warrington this time. They've slowed down, though. It's the one advantage of Rachel causing such a lot of grief. Mum's too busy worrying about her to fuss over some sick pervert.

19 April, 1995

Rachel's been called as a witness – for the other side. The Crown Prosecution Service wants her to give evidence AGAINST us. David and Jean Crosbie came over together to tell us. Mum, Sinbad and I just sat there when we heard, not able to say a thing. Mum couldn't take it in at first. She kept asking why, then saying she didn't believe it.

It's true though. David Crosbie showed us the letter Rachel got. When Mum took it over to her the other day, she assumed it was something about school. I wish!

It was like someone had hit me right in the chest. I couldn't breathe for shock. My eyes wouldn't move. They just focused on Mum's hankie, staring at the white material snaking in and out of grey fingers.

David and Jean left without even a cup of tea. After a while, the three of us unfroze enough to talk about it. It was easy enough to work out why the CPS has called Rachel. The detectives told us ages ago that she told them Dad never laid a finger on us.

I know he did. Mum knows he did, but Rachel says he didn't. That's why they've called her. To make out we're lying.

Mum's so naïve. Surely, Rachel wouldn't tell lies against us!

Oh no? She won't even talk to us. Every chance she gets she shouts and screams to the world about how much she hates us and wants us to go to prison for ever. A few little lies in the dock won't worry her.

There's no way we can stop her. From now on, we can't have any contact with her at all. We're completely done for. Who's going to doubt the word of an innocent sixteen-year-old? If the prosecution's called her against us, that's that. We'll be two liars in the dock who killed a man for no reason.

21 April, 1995

I've just checked back – it's been almost a week since we got any hate mail. They've stopped at last. Whoever's writing them has found somebody else to persecute. Mum's worried that they're going to start again once the trial begins.

She's getting herself into a state. Over the past couple of weeks, she was doing really well, what with the baby and everything. Now, we're right back to doom and despair. If only she'd try and be positive. She's got to pull herself together. Concentrate on having our say in court and walking out free.

The baby should be one of the good things, but Mum's worried to death about it. Should we tell our solicitor? Sinbad wanted to keep it quiet. The prosecution barristers are bound to make something of it.

Dad gets killed.

Sinbad buys the house.

Mum gets pregnant.

Doesn't look too good!!!

Mum and Sinbad argued about it for hours. The

whole discussion was completely pointless! Every single neighbour knows she's pregnant, so we can hardly keep the forces of law from finding out.

Besides, it's not going to be a problem. All we've got to do is tell the truth.

Mum's getting a fixation about talking to Rachel. Even though she knows we're not supposed to contact her now she's a witness for the prosecution. Rachel literally runs away the moment she sets eyes on us. It's so hard for Mum. Rachel's still her daughter, no matter what she's going to say in court.

22 April, 1995

We had to see the solicitor again today. It was a long meeting! First of all, we had to go through the transcripts of our interviews with the police, to make sure we both agreed with the statements we made.

Mum went white when she heard that. It's like they're forcing us to relive it over and over again. Alison Dicks made us go through every paragraph, every line, every word, every comma and every full stop. What did we mean by this? Was it forced out of us? Why did we say that? Especially when we lied! You'd've thought people would realize why I was trying to protect Mum and vice versa, but no! It seems it's not going to look good in court.

I don't know what good it did. I know exactly where we stand and exactly what I want to tell the courts.

There's nothing dodgy about the statements. The police didn't add or take away anything. I hadn't realized before quite how long we'd spent in that dingy little room, pouring out hearts out to Detective Inspector Coban. But there's nothing I'm ashamed of. Once I stopped trying to cover up for Mum, I told the absolute truth. And I'll say it again in court!

By the time we'd finished, Mum looked absolutely washed out. Then, Alison smiled and relaxed a bit. What a hypocrite! She believed congratulations were in order on Mum's pregnancy!!

It was obvious how she found out. Rachel told the prosecution's solicitor and he told ours. Friendly of him! Ms. Dicks wasn't happy about it. We're supposed to tell her everything if she's going to defend us. She says she's on our side, but I don't quite trust her.

Especially when we went on to talk about strategies and tactics. Our barrister's Paul Anderson QC. Apparently, he's got a good reputation for handling domestic violence cases. His idea is that Mum should plead guilty to manslaughter on the grounds of diminished responsibility. That means the conspiracy charges may be dropped and Mum would be up for a much shorter sentence, or even a suspended one. Plea-bargaining – that's what they call it in America. Strategies and tactics? Whatever happened to the truth? Is this a justice system or what?

Mum's not pleading guilty to anything. We did what we did because it had to be done and that's what I want to tell the court. I don't want any clever-dick barrister persuading us to go against what's the truth. Mum didn't have diminished responsibility. She had no choice. Neither of us did. I don't want any of these legal games. We're pleading not guilty. It wasn't murder. It was self-defence.

I suppose I was shouting a bit, but that Alison Dicks really laid into me. I'm not allowed to say what I want, because the prosecution will be trying to make me lose my cool every inch of the way. They'll make me out to be the aggressive little murderer who flies off the handle at the drop of a hat. I'll be playing right into their hands.

Why does it have to be such a game? I don't know if I can play it their way. Why should we have to pretend to be mad to get justice? We can't we just tell the truth?

23 April, 1995

I've been thinking all night about what Alison said. It's so unfair! Even worse, I'm not sure I can keep my temper. I get so wound up inside, I can't keep my mouth shut and stay sweet and nice and pleasant. Like a well-brought up young lady should be! I've got to seem to be something I'm not. Highlight the earnest medical student, play down the lesbian. Be cool – but not too cool, or they'll think you're a heartless bitch! Shed a few tears, but not too many, or they'll think you're an unstable neurotic.

I don't care. I'll tell them just what an animal my father was. That he deserved to die for what he did to us. If there's any justice in the world, we'll be set free. He kept us locked away long enough. We're not going down without a fright. We were right to do what we did and the court's got to be made to see that.

I'm terrified of what Rachel will say. The whole of our defence rests on what he was like. She's going to make out he was the ideal dad. She just can't admit to herself what he did to her. What chance is there of getting her to tell the truth in court?

One of us has got to talk to her. Get her to tell the truth. There's no other option. I don't care if I get into trouble. What could be worse than facing a life sentence for murder? What are they going to do? Fine me as well?

I discussed it with Sinbad. He was dead against me going anywhere near Rachel. I had to give in. If the thought of me confronting her was doing Sinbad's head in, I dread to think what it would do to Mum. But what are we supposed to do? Stand back and let her tell a pack of lies about her wonderful dad? We're finished!

My sister makes me sick. She's playing the little goody-goody now. David Crosbie has persuaded her to go back to school. Who the hell does he think he is? It's got nothing to do with him.

Sinbad actually fells sorry for him. Poor man! Stuck in the middle of World War Three!! My heart bleeds. Meanwhile, we're facing life imprisonment with nobody to stand up in court for us.

24 April, 1995

TWO WEEKS TODAY!!!

Try not to think about it.

Another perfect day in Paradise. I look like death warmed up. I can't eat. I can't sleep. Even breathing's an effort. It's like I'm keyed up the whole time and utterly exhausted.

Mum's no help. She's worse than I am. Just when she should be taking it easy and getting plenty of rest. At this rate, she could have a miscarriage or something. Her weight's gone down because she won't eat anything. It's like she's completely lost hope.

In the end I went round to see Mike at Jacqui and Katie's. Not that I was exactly good company! He was really sweet, telling me about all these women who got off who had been up on similar charges. I don't know who he was trying to convince – me or himself! Still, it makes a change to have a bit of support. Since Rachel's been round at the Crosbies, we haven't had a chance to have a proper talk with Jean. All she can do is sneak out, give us a two second progress check, and sneak back again.

Mike was horrified when I told him how things stood. He'd assumed we had a good chance of getting off on the grounds of self-defence. But that's not the way the prosecution's going to play it. They'll say we planned it. Killed him in cold blood. Premeditated.

I told him about Rachel being called as a witness.

And about the abuse. He almost broke down in tears when I'd finished. He couldn't believe we would be banged up when the court heard about that. It was obvious to everyone what he was like.

But it's not that simple! Who really saw what he was like? Witnessed actual events? The court's only going to listen to people who were there, on the spot. There was only Rachel and she's denied all along that anything happened. It won't be any different now.

I ended up sobbing in Mike's arms. Of course, Jacqui would have to choose that moment to come in. She looked furious at finding me there. Yet another person who hates me!

26 April, 1995

I thought they'd stopped! We got the worst piece of hate mail yet this morning. It was longer than the others and bulky, like there was something enclosed with it. At first I thought it was a letter of support. The writer started off by saying he or she sympathized with our predicament, but there was a way out.

Sellotaped to the second page were sixteen capsules. They were labelled – SLEEPING PILLS. Underneath was written DIY DEATH PENALTY. It was all I could do to keep from being sick. After everything that's happened, I think this was the most shocking.

Sinbad ripped the pills from my hand, and flushed them down the toilet.

In less than two weeks, we're going to get our chance to tell the world OUR side of the story. So far the police, the press and the perverts have had it all their own way. We'll set the record straight and we'll be freed.

When I had another look at the letter, I realized it was from the same person as the others, only posted in Preston this time.

Mike came round again. I told him about the hate mail. He looked gobsmacked. I thought he was going to faint, he was so white. But he had something else on his mind.

He volunteered to be a witness for the defence. I didn't get what he was going on about to start with. He never witnessed anything to do with us and Dad.

Mike's prepared to lie for us. He'd got his story worked out – how he knocked for me one day, but got no answer, so he went round the back and saw Dad on top of me. I was really choked. I don't know whether I was more touched or embarrassed. After all that's happened between us, he's still a completely loyal friend.

Of course, I wouldn't let him do it. He could get done for perjury. No way is he going to risk that for me. Even if I could get locked away for life. I'll never be able to tell how much it means to me to have his support.

27 April, 1995

I thought we'd scraped the barrel with this hate mail, but this latest piece of spite is unbelievable. Someone sent us a mass card. Hand-delivered this time.

RIP
BETH AND MANDY JORDACHE

It's sick and it's twisted. How could anyone have the nerve? Mike came round again, so I showed him the disgusting thing. Something was wrong. He couldn't look me in the eye. It took me ages to get the truth out of him.

Jacqui Dixon's the one holding the poison pen. Mike got suspicious when I told him yesterday how they were a mixture of hand-delivered and posted in various towns round here. It seems Jacqui's been going round car boot sales lately. And the last one was in Preston – same as the postmark on the letter with the sleeping pills. This morning she called in sick, so it would have been easy for her to deliver the mass card. The final straw for Mike was when he caught her secretly writing a letter. He'd hardly ever seen her put pen to paper before AND she shoved the paper under a book as soon as he came in.

I should have guessed. It fits in perfectly with the way she feels about me. She never misses a chance to have a go at me. I can't believe she could be so vicious and vindictive to me! What have I ever done to her?

Even when I was staying at her flat, she was a right cow. She's stuffed full of prejudices. Just because I'm gay, she thinks it means I'm the most evil person in the world.

I was too angry to sit still. Mike tried to stop me when he saw how furious I was. We don't have any rock solid proof, he didn't recognize the handwriting, etc. etc. Obviously she disguised it. What more proof do we need?

No way was I going to cool down. I slammed out of the house with Mike on my heels. Lucky for her she was out. So much for her being on the sick! Probably out sending more poisonous post.

It's only a matter of time before I catch up with her. If she *is* the one behind it, she'll regret it when I do.

28 April, 1995

Mum's lost her nerve! We had to have yet another meeting with Alison Dicks this morning, going over the same stuff we discussed last time. And the time before. Mum wouldn't even get out of bed. She's had it with everybody looking at her all the time and talking behind our backs. As far as she's concerned, we don't stand a chance in court, so there was no point in seeing the solicitor.

Sinbad and I had to wrestle the duvet away from her. It was utterly ridiculous! Still, Mum's negative attitude made me feel even more determined to show the world what we're made of.

All the same, going to the solicitors was just another pointless, boring repetition of what we already knew.

When we got back, I took Sinbad to one side and told him about Jacqui Dixon. It took me ages to convince him it could be her. When I had, he was all for going round to Ron Dixon's and getting him to sort it out. Fat lot of good that'd do! I'm hardly his favourite person. He'd most likely pat Jacqui on the back and tell her to carry on the good work!

No! I'm going to fight my own battles.

I finally ran Jacqui to earth on the Close, as she was leaving Patricia's place. She denied it completely, of course. Pretended not to recognize the sleeping pill letter or the mass card. Even when I told her Mike had seen her actually writing one of the letters, she claimed not to know what I was talking about. I had to spell it out to her in words of one syllable.

I have to admit, she really looked as if it came as a total surprise to her. Then, she admitted what she'd been writing when Mike caught her. It was a letter to the judge, telling him that Mike was going to lie for us about seeing me and Dad! She said she couldn't care less where *I* ended up, but she wasn't about to let her own brother risk going to jail. If only Rachel felt like that about me!

I've probably made a complete fool of myself.

So what? It's not like I can blacken the family name any more.

I talked it over with Sinbad. The trouble is – I think I believe her. Sinbad does as well. I was so convinced it was her, I don't know what to think now.

It has to be someone who knows us. Someone from round here. Someone who hates me more than Jacqui Dixon does.

Why didn't I realize before? There *is* someone else, who fits the description exactly. And he was in Preston last week, helping Jacqui with the car boot sale. It must the moral crusader himself – David Crosbie.

29 April, 1995

Sinbad and I were having another tussle to get Mum out of bed this morning, when I spotted David Crosbie sneaking across to our letter box. I couldn't believe it! I dashed downstairs to catch him at it. Sure enough, there was a note lying on the mat. Hand-delivered.

I got to the door so quickly, he was still standing on the door-step. I opened the letter in front of him – and could have fallen through the floorboards. It was an invitation to a street party next week. VE Day! To celebrate the end of a war!!

Another embarrassing mistake! Mr. Crosbie was really offended and hurt. When I took a good look at the note, it obviously wasn't from the hate-mailer. The handwriting and the ink were totally different. I never thought I'd feel ashamed of having a go at him, but I wasn't even thinking straight. This business is getting to me in a big way. He and Jean are on our side – I know that. Besides, he's always been up front about what he thinks. He hasn't exactly been afraid to have a go at me. Why should he suddenly start sending anonymous letters?

Whoever's sending these letters hasn't got the guts to show their face. They can do what they like. We're not going to be scared off. We're innocent.

5 May, 1995

Alison Dicks has made Mum go to see a psychiatrist, to help to put a defence case together. It's so unfair. Why do we need a psychiatrist's report? Why can't we just tell the truth, instead of it sounding like we were insane or whatever when we did it. We should just be able to plead self-defence. Mum wasn't out of her mind when she killed him. She did it because we were scared for our lives. He'd threatened to kill us and he meant it. Self-defence. There's no other way of putting it.

Mum, agreed immediately of course. They're the professionals. They know best. Like the police and the prison officers and the probation service that let Dad out to come and terrorize us.

Alison Dicks is still harping on about diminished responsibility. Our plan of attack is to convince the jury that Dad's physical, mental and sexual abuse provoked Mum until she was at breaking point, i.e., she was no longer responsible for her actions. That's basically what diminished responsibility means – proving you were mad to do what you did.

Diminished responsibility? That's a laugh. Getting rid of him was the most responsible thing we've ever done. The years of abuse we put up with! The fists, the groping. The rape. And she wants Mum to go into the witness box and pretend she's mad!

We should be telling the judge and jury that he tortured us until killing him was the only way out. I'm scared that they'll end up locking Mum away in some mental institution. Then she really *would* be locked away for ever.

It's the world that's gone mad, not us. Jimmy Corkhill was round here, offering to pay for us to get away. He's got a car lined up for us with a full tank of petrol. False passports? No problem! I couldn't take it seriously. Until I realized what he really wanted. The house! He was going to buy it off Sinbad for a pittance. That man is such a leech. I threw him straight out.

7 May, 1995

Mum and I had a row this evening. It was so stupid! Aunt Brenna turned up from Ireland. Being Dad's sister, she could never see anything wrong with him. She wheedled her way into the Crosbies', where Rachel was only too pleased to see her. Then, she actually got in here! I couldn't believe Mum let her in. Sinbad caught her giving Mum a really hard time, trying to persuade her to plead guilty and 'stop saying those awful things'. All the old arguments – for Rachel's sake, for Trevor's. It was for Rachel's sake that we got into this mess in the first place. And we don't owe that man a thing!

Sinbad threw her out.

When I heard what'd happened, I lost it yet again. What the hell was Mum thinking of, letting her in? I can't even go out for a couple of hours. What is it with her? Why can't she stand up for herself? Do I have to do everything?

I regretted it as soon as I opened my mouth. I'm sick and tired of the whole business. We all are. Why did Brenna have to turn up now? One of our last nights together and Mum and I were almost at each other's throats.

Sinbad made us calm down. He cooked us a meal – straight out of a tin! Still, it made us laugh. Jean came round with a bunch of flowers to wish us luck. I was actually starting to relax when something came through the letter box. It was another bit of hate mail.

I'LL BE IN COURT WATCHING YOU.
YOU'RE GOING TO PRISON.
ROT IN HELL.

I was scared to death. I suddenly remembered the video diary I'd made last year. It's just been lying around all this time. Talk about incriminating evidence. Supposing someone got hold of it? Even if we did get off, it might be enough to get the case reopened or something.

Then I had a brilliant idea. I went round to Mike's to borrow his camera again. In a week or so, Mum and I might be facing a lifetime behind bars. I may never see her again. What's going to happen to my new brother or sister?

Instead of the story of a murder, the tape's got a video letter to Mum and Sinbad's baby. I went into the nursery and told him or her about all the good things. One day, we'll meet. If there's any justice in the world, it'll be at the birth. If not, then when we get out. Even if Mum and I get sent down, we'll survive. Somehow. I'm never going to give up. We had to do it . . . It was him or us . . .